The Mystery of Cloomber

Sir Arthur Conan Doyle

With a New Introduction by
Mike Ashley

DOVER PUBLICATIONS, INC.
Mineola, New York

Bibliographical Note

This Dover edition, first published in 2009, is an unabridged republication
of the work published in 1895 by R. F. Fenno & Company, New York. A
new Introduction by Mike Ashley has been specially prepared for the
Dover edition.

Library of Congress Cataloging-in-Publication Data

Doyle, Arthur Conan, Sir, 1859–1930.

  The mystery of Cloomber / Sir Arthur Conan Doyle ; with a new
introduction by Mike Ashley.

    p. cm.

  ISBN-13: 978-0-486-47357-4

  ISBN-10: 0-486-47357-0

  1. Wigtownshire (Scotland)—Fiction.   2. East India Company.
Army—Officers—Fiction.   3. Hindu Kush Mountains Region
(Afghanistan and Pakistan)—Fiction.   4. Massacres—
Fiction.   5. Buddhist priests—Fiction.   6. Revenge—
Fiction.   I. Title.

  PR4622.M9   2009

  823′.8—dc22

                                                        2009029290

Manufactured in the United States by Courier Corporation

47357001

www.doverpublications.com

INTRODUCTION

THE TWO SIDES OF SIR ARTHUR CONAN DOYLE

by Mike Ashley

The Mystery of Cloomber is Sir Arthur Conan Doyle's forgotten novel. It was his second to be published (first serialized in the *Pall Mall Gazette*, and then published by Ward and Downey in 1888). It followed the Sherlock Holmes adventure *A Study in Scarlet*, but with Conan Doyle's own desire to write historical novels and the public's growing desire for more Holmes, his early writings were soon forgotten. Conan Doyle himself grew dissatisfied with *Cloomber*, and it faded into oblivion. Yet, in considering the direction that Conan Doyle's fiction took, the novel was a pivotal work.

At the start of *The Hound of the Baskervilles*, probably the best known and most famous of all the Sherlock Holmes works, Holmes is faced with a dilemma. Is the fiendish hound of supernatural or natural origin? The detective states, "[if] ... we are dealing with forces outside the ordinary laws of Nature, there is an end of our investigation." Holmes, the most methodical and rational of all detectives, actually concedes there could be laws beyond Nature. Admittedly, he also remarks, "The devil's agents may be of flesh and blood, may they not?"—bringing us to the very nub of Conan Doyle's own dilemma.

For much of his life, and certainly the second half, Conan Doyle was a confirmed spiritualist, a believer in the afterlife and all that it entailed. Yet, in the character of Sherlock Holmes, he had created a human being so rational in his outlook that he would always look for the human agency in his crimes, never the supernatural. So, to satisfy his interest in the supernatural, Conan Doyle wrote ghost stories, weird tales, and horror stories.

If it had not been for the success of Sherlock Holmes, Conan Doyle might well have been best remembered as a writer of supernatural fiction, ranked alongside his contemporaries M. R. James, Arthur Machen, and Algernon Blackwood.

Conan Doyle himself most wanted to write historical fiction, and although he had moderate success with *Micah Clarke*, *The White Company*, and the Brigadier Gerard stories, these took time to write and research. The Holmes stories also took longer and longer to plot. Conan Doyle may have been paid handsomely for the result, but it wasn't what he wanted to do. And, early in his career, it did not pay the bills.

Conan Doyle delighted in basic adventure stories and thrillers—"boy's own" potboilers that stirred, even chilled the blood, creating that frisson of excitement, and they could be written quickly and easily for rapid, if modest, financial return. He would even regale his fellow pupils at Stonyhurst College with lurid tales in return for cakes and sweets. The very first story he submitted for publication, "The Haunted Grange of Goresthorpe," may well have been one of those tales, as it's a first-person account of an encounter with a ghost.

Thus, a high proportion of Conan Doyle's early story sales drew upon supernatural or other legends. His first published story, "The Mystery of Sasassa Valley" (1879), dates from the period when Conan Doyle was a medical student in Edinburgh; it concerns a valley in South Africa believed to be inhabited by a demon with glowing eyes. "The Captain of the 'Polestar'" (1883), the first story of which Conan Doyle was proud, tells of a ship in Arctic waters whose captain is lured to his death by the spirit of a dead woman. In similar fashion, a beautiful woman has a mesmerizing power of life or death over men in "John Barrington Cowles" (1886). "The Great Keinplatz Experiment" (1885), also uses hypnotism to show how there could be a transfer of minds between individuals. "The Silver Hatchet" (1883) is of particular interest because it deals with a small hatchet used in a murder that was cursed, so that all who held it turned homicidal—it had become a means of revenge.

Conan Doyle achieved a singular triumph with "J. Habakuk Jephson's Statement," which was published anonymously in *The*

Cornhill Magazine in 1884. This work dealt with the fate of the crew of the *Marie Celeste,* and Conan Doyle's explanation was so convincing that many believed the story to be true (it was Conan Doyle who effectively created and popularized the legend of the *Marie Celeste*). Conan Doyle was good at creating legends—not only Sherlock Holmes, but also the concept of the Lost World, in which prehistoric monsters might survive. In "The Los Amigos Fiasco," an 1892 short story, although presented in a humorous tone, Conan Doyle offered the idea that some criminals might not die when executed in the electric chair; rather, the surge of electricity might make them immortal. It was an idea that some half-believed at the time. So Conan Doyle rapidly developed a style, through his first person narrative and by tapping into what people were willing to believe, that created stories that made the supernatural acceptable.

During the 1880s he worked through his literary apprenticeship, and by 1887 he was prepared to tackle a full-length work. It is fascinating that his first two novels, *A Study in Scarlet* and *The Mystery of Cloomber*, can almost be viewed as two sides of the same coin. On the one side, we find the ultimate rationalist, Sherlock Holmes, but on the other we see the irrationalist, whose belief systems and uncertainty persuade us to accept the impossible.

Both novels are tales of revenge, and both involve various religious beliefs. There are many other similarities: *A Study in Scarlet* involves the murder of two former Mormons who had been involved in the death of a young girl and her father. Holmes reveals that the word RACHE, written above the body of the first murder victim, is German for "revenge." The story is told in two distinct parts, the first following Holmes's investigation, but the second offering an account of a back-story that reveals the full motive behind the murders. *A Study in Scarlet* also relates the first meeting between Sherlock Holmes and Dr. John Watson, and we learn about Watson's past, including his time spent in the army in India and in the Afghan War.

Bear these facts in mind when reading *The Mystery of Cloomber*. Without revealing too much, the story is recounted by John West (his first name and initials similar to Watson's),

who encounters John Berthier Heatherstone, the owner of
Cloomber Hall and a former general in the Indian Army. During his service, he had committed a sin against a religious sect.
Heatherstone and his companion, Colonel Rufus Smith, are
destined to meet their fate by way of revenge, as related in the
second part of the book, revealed in old papers. Although this
fate may be delivered by a human agency, the novel is perme-
ated by an inevitability of forces beyond human ken. In addition, many of Conan Doyle's early stories are told in the first
person—in this way, the author and the reader instantly embed
themselves in the narrative. *The Mystery of Cloomber* is no exception to this effective technique.

Evidently, at this time, Conan Doyle was wrestling between
writing novels of a very methodical, human world and those of
an inexplicable, darker world—the world he had already been
exploring in his short stories. As a novice writer, he used the
same method and approach to both books, creating in *The Mystery of Cloomber* a dark alternative to *A Study in Scarlet.*

We know, in retrospect, how Conan Doyle's "future" unrav-
elled. The success of Sherlock Holmes meant that Conan Doyle
was compelled, in the end, to follow the methodical route. He
still found opportunities to return to the supernatural in his
short stories, and even brought a hint of it into Holmes's world
in *The Hound of the Baskervilles.* Eventually, Conan Doyle was
able to return to it in full force in the Professor Challenger stories, beginning with *The Lost World* and including the very
sinister spiritualist novel *The Land of Mist.*

Thus the two competing sides of Conan Doyle tussled
throughout his writing career, and the present edition, *The Mystery of Cloomber*, marks where those two sides first split. In
spite of its signs of being an early work—Conan Doyle actually
started it in 1883 but did not finish it until after *A Study in Scarlet* in 1888—and certain inaccuracies regarding the Buddhist,
Hindu, and Islamic religions, the book deserves to be restored
to its rightful place in Sir Arthur Conan Doyle's development as
a writer.

CONTENTS

The Mystery of Cloomber

CHAPTER I

I, JOHN FOTHERGILL WEST, student of law in the University of St. Andrews, have endeavored in the ensuing pages to lay my statement before the public in a concise and business-like fashion. It is not my wish to achieve literary success; nor have I any desire by the graces of my style, or by the artistic ordering of my incidents, to throw a deeper shadow over the strange passages of which I shall have to speak. My highest ambition is that those who know something of the matter should, after reading my account, be able to conscientiously endorse it without finding a single paragraph in which I have either added to or detracted from the truth. Should I attain this result, I shall rest amply satisfied with the outcome of my first, and probably my last, venture in literature.

It was my intention to write out the sequence of events in due order, depending upon trustworthy hearsay when I was describing that which was beyond my own personal knowledge. I have now, however, through the kind co-operation of friends, hit upon a plan which promises to be less onerous to me and more satisfactory to the reader. This is nothing less than to make use of the various manuscripts which I have by me bearing upon the subject, and to add to them first-hand evidence contributed by those who had the best opportunities of knowing Major-General J. B. Heatherstone. In pursuance of this design I shall lay before the public the testimony of Israel Stakes, formerly coachman at Cloomber Hall, and of John Easterling, F. R. C. P. Edin., now practising at Stranraer, in Wigtownshire. To these I shall add a

1

verbatim account extracted from the journal of the late John Berthier Heatherstone, of the events which occurred in the Thul Valley in the autumn of '41, towards the end of the first Afghan war, with a description of the skirmish in the Terada defile, and of the death of the man Ghoolab Shah. To myself I reserve the duty of filling up all the gaps and chinks which may be left in the narrative. By this arrangement I have sunk from the position of an author to that of a compiler, but on the other hand my work has ceased to be a story and has expanded into a series of affidavits.

My father, John Hunter West, was a well-known Oriental and Sanscrit scholar, and his name is still of weight with those who are interested in such matters. He it was who first after Sir William Jones called attention to the great value of early Persian literature, and his translations both from Hafiz and from Ferid-eddin Atar have earned the warmest commendations from the Baron Von Hammer-Purgstall, of Vienna, and other distinguished Continental critics. In the issue of the *Orientalisches Scienz-blatt* for January, 1861, he is described as "Der beruhmte und sehr gelehrnte Hunter West von Edinburgh"—a passage which I well remember that he cut out and stowed away, with a pardonable vanity, among the most revered family archives.

He has been brought up to be a solicitor, or Writer to the Signet, as it is termed in Scotland, but his learned hobby absorbed so much of his time that he had little to devote to the pursuit of his profession. When his clients were seeking him at his chambers in George Street he was buried in the recesses of the Advocates' Library, or poring over some mouldy manuscript at the Philosophical Institution, with his brain more exercised over the code which Menu pro-pounded six hundred years before the birth of Christ than over the knotty problems of Scottish law in the nineteenth century.

Hence it can hardly be wondered at that as his learning accumulated his practise dissolved, until at the very moment when he had attained the zenith of his celebrity he had also reached the nadir of his fortunes. There being no chair of Sanscrit in any of his native universities, and no demand anywhere for the only mental wares he had to dispose of, we should have been forced

to retire into genteel poverty, consoling ourselves with the aphorisms and precepts of Firdousi, Omar Chiam, and other of his
Eastern favorites, had it not been for the unexpected kindness
had liberality of his half-brother, William Farintosh, the Laird of
Branksome in Wigtownshire.

This William Farintosh was the proprietor of a landed estate
the acreage of which bore, unfortunately, a most disproportional
relation to its value, for it formed the bleakest and most barren
tract of land in the whole of a bleak and barren shire. As a bach-
elor, however, his expenses had been small, and he had con-
trived from the rents of his scattered cottages, and the sale of
the Galloway nags, which he bred upon the moors, not only to
live as a laird should, but to put by a considerable sum in the
bank.

We had heard little from our kinsman during the days of our
comparative prosperity; but just as we were at our wits' end,
there came a letter like a ministering angel, giving us assurance
of sympathy and succor. In it the Laird of Branksome told us
that one of his lungs had been growing weaker for some time,
and that Dr. Easterling, of Stranraer, had strongly advised him
to spend the few years which were left to him in some more
genial climate. He had determined, therefore, to set out for the
South of Italy, and he begged that we should take up our residence at Branksome in his absence, and that my father should
act as his land steward and agent at a salary which placed us
above all fear of want.

Our mother had been dead for some years, so that there were
only myself, my father, and my sister Esther to consult; and it
may readily be imagined that it did not take us long to decide
upon the acceptance of the laird's generous offer. My father
started for Wigtown that very night, while Esther and I followed
a few days afterwards, bearing with us two potato-sacks full of
learned books, and such other of our household effects as were
worth the trouble and expense of transport.

CHAPTER II

BRANKSOME might have appeared a poor dwelling-place when compared to the house of an English squire; but to us, after our long residence in stuffy apartments, it was of regal magnificence. The building was broadspread and low, with red-tiled roof, diamond-paned windows, and a profusion of dining-rooms with smoke-blackened ceilings and oaken wainscots. In front was a small lawn, girt round with a thin fringe of haggard and ill-grown beeches, all gnarled and withered from the blighting effects of the sea spray. Behind lay the scattered hamlet of Branksome-Bere—a dozen cottages at most—inhabited by rude fisher-folk who looked upon the laird as their natural protector. To the west was the broad yellow beach and the Irish Sea; while in all other directions the desolate moors, greyish green in the foreground and purple in the distance, stretched away in long, low curves to the horizon.

Very bleak and lonely it was upon this Wigtown coast. A man might walk many a weary mile and never see a living thing except the white, heavy-flapping kittiwakes, which screamed and cried to each other with their shrill, sad voices. Very lonely and very bleak! Once out of sight of Branksome and there was no sign of the works of man save only where the high, white tower of Cloomber Hall shot up, like the headstone of some giant grave, from amid the firs and larches which girt it round. This great house, a mile or more from our dwelling, had been built by a wealthy Glasgow merchant of strange tastes and lonely habits; but at the time of our arrival it had been untenanted for many years, and stood with weather-blotched walls and vacant, staring windows looking blankly out over the hill side. Empty and mildewed, it served only as a landmark to the fishermen, for they had found by experience that by keeping the laird's chimney and the white tower of Cloomber in a line they could steer their way through the ugly reef which raises its jagged back, like that of some sleeping monster, above the troubled waters of the wind-swept bay.

To this wild spot it was that fate had brought my father, my sister, and myself. For us its loneliness had no terrors. After the hubbub and bustle of a great city, and the weary task of upholding appearances upon a slender income, there was a grand, soul-soothing serenity in the long sky-line and the eager air. Here at least there was no neighbor to pry and chatter. The laird had left his phaeton and two ponies behind him, with the aid of which my father and I would go the round of the estate doing such light duties as fall to an agent; while our gentle Esther looked to our household needs, and brightened the dark old building. Such was our simple, uneventful existence until the summer night when an unlooked-for incident occurred which proved to be the herald of those strange doings which I have taken up my pen to describe.

It had been my habit to pull out of an evening in the laird's skiff and to catch a few whiting which might serve for our supper. On this well-remembered occasion my sister came with me, sitting with her book in the stern-sheets of the boat, while I hung my lines over the bows. The sun had sunk down behind the rugged Irish coast, but a long bank of flushed clouds still marked the spot, and cast a glory upon the waters. The whole broad ocean was seamed and scarred with crimson streaks. I had risen in the boat, and was gazing round in delight at the broad panorama of shore and sea and sky, when my sister plucked at any sleeve with a little, sharp cry of surprise.

"See, John," she cried; "there is a light in Cloomber Tower!"

I turned my head and stared back at the tall, white turret which peeped out above the belt of trees. As I gazed I distinctly saw at one of the windows the glint of a light, which suddenly vanished, and then shone out once more from another higher up. There it flickered for some time, and finally flashed past two successive windows underneath before the trees obscured our view of it. It was clear that some one bearing a lamp or a candle had climbed up the tower stairs and had then returned into the body of the house.

"Who in the world can it be!" I exclaimed, speaking rather to myself than to Esther, for I could see by the surprise upon her face that she had no solution to offer. "Maybe some of the folk from Branksome-Bere have wanted to look over the place."

My sister shook her head. "There is not one of them would dare to set foot within the avenue gates," she said. "Besides, John, the keys are kept by the house-agent at Wigtown. Were they ever so curious, none of our people could find their way in."

When I reflected upon the massive door and ponderous shutters which guarded the lower story of Cloomber I could not but admit the force of my sister's objection. The untimely visitor must either have used considerable violence in order to force his way in, or he must have obtained possession of the keys. Piqued by the little mystery, I pulled for the beach, with the determination to see for myself who the intruder might be, and what were his intentions. Leaving my sister at Branksome, and summoning Seth Jamieson, an old man-o'-war's-man, and one of the stoutest of the fishermen, I set off across the moor with him through the gathering darkness.

"It hasna got a guid name after dark, yon hoose," remarked my companion, slackening his pace perceptibly as I explained to him the nature of our errand. "It's no for naething that him wha owns it wunna gang within a Scotch mile o't."

"Well, Seth, there is some one who has no fears about going into it," said I, pointing to the great, white building which flickered up in front of us through the gloom. The light which I had observed from the sea was moving backwards and forwards past the lower-floor windows, the shutters of which had been removed. I could now see that a second, fainter light followed a few paces behind the other. Evidently two individuals, the one with a lamp and the other with a candle or rushlight, were making a careful examination of the building.

"Let ilka man blaw his ain parritch," said Seth Jamieson, doggedly, coming to a dead stop. "What is it tae us if a wraith or a

bogle chooses tae tak' a fancy tae Cloomber? It's no canny tae
meddle wi' such things."

"Why, man," I cried, "you don't suppose a wraith came here
in a gig! What are those lights away yonder by the avenue
gates?"

"The lamps o' a gig, sure enough!" exclaimed my companion
in a less lugubrious voice. "Let's steer for it, Master West, and
speer where she hails frae."

By this time night had closed in save for a single long, narrow
slit in the westward. Stumbling across the moor together, we
made our way into the Wigtown Road, at the point where the
high, stone pillars mark the entrance to the Cloomber avenue.
A tall dog-cart stood in front of the gateway, the horse browsing
upon the thin border of grass which skirted the road.

"It's a' richt!" said Jamieson, taking a close look at the deserted vehicle. "I ken it weel. It belongs tae Maister McNeil, the
factor body frae Wigtown—him who keeps the keys."

"Then we may as well have speech with him now that we are
here," I answered. "They are coming down, if I am not mistaken." As I spoke we heard the slam of the heavy door, and
within a few minutes two figures, the one tall and angular, the
other short and thick, came towards us through the darkness.
They were talking so earnestly that they did not observe us until
they had passed through the avenue gate.

"Good evening, Mr. McNeil," said I, stepping forward and
addressing the Wigtown factor, with whom I had some slight
acquaintance. The smaller of the two turned his face towards
me as I spoke, and showed me that I was not mistaken in his
identity, but his taller companion sprang back and showed every
sign of violent agitation.

"What is this, McNeil?" I heard him say, in a gasping, choking
voice. "Is this your promise? What is the meaning of it?"

"Don't be alarmed, general! Don't be alarmed!" said the little,
fat factor in a soothing fashion, as one might speak to a frightened child. "This is young Mr. Fothergill West, of Branksome,
though what brings him up here to-night is more than I can
understand. However, as you are to be neighbors, I can't do better than take the opportunity to introduce you to each other. Mr.

West, this is General Heatherstone, who is about to take a lease of Cloomber Hall.

I held out my hand to the tall man, who took it in a hesitating, half-reluctant fashion. "I came up," I explained, "because I saw your lights in the windows, and thought that something might be wrong. I am very glad I did so, since it has given me the chance of making the general's acquaintance."

Whilst I was talking I was conscious that the new tenant of Cloomber Hall was peering at me very closely through the darkness. As I concluded he stretched out a long, tremulous arm and turned the gig-lamp in such a way as to throw a flood of light on my face.

"Good God, McNeil!" he cried, in the same frightened voice as before, "the fellow's as brown as chocolate! He's not an Englishman. You're not an Englishman—you, sir?"

"I'm a Scotchman, born and bred," said I, with an inclination to laugh, which was only checked by my new acquaintance's obvious terror.

"A Scotchman, eh?" said he with a sigh of relief. "It's all one nowadays. You must excuse me, Mr.—Mr. West. I'm nervous, infernally nervous. Come along, McNeil; we must be back in Wigtown in less than an hour. Good-night, gentlemen, good-night!" The two clambered into their places; the factor cracked his whip, and the high dog-cart clattered away through the darkness, casting a brilliant tunnel of yellow light on either side of it, until the rumble of its wheels died away in the distance.

"What do you think of our new neighbor, Jamieson?" I asked, after a long silence.

"Deed, Mr. West, he seems, as he says himself, to be vera nervous. Maybe his conscience is oot o' order."

"His liver, more likely," said I. "He looks as if he had tried his constitution a bit. But it's blowing chill, Seth, my lad, and it's time both of us were indoors." I bade my companion good-night, and struck off across the moors for the cherry, ruddy light which marked the parlor windows of Branksome.

CHAPTER III

OF OUR FURTHER ACQUAINTANCE WITH MAJOR-GENERAL J. B. HEATHERSTONE

THERE was, as may well be imagined, much stir amongst our small community at the news that the Hall was to be inhabited once more, and considerable speculation as to the new tenants and their objects in choosing this particular part of the country for their residence. It speedily became apparent that, whatever their motives might be, they had definitely determined upon a lengthy stay; for relays of plumbers and of joiners came down from Wigtown, and there was hammering and repairing going on from morning till night. It was surprising how quick the signs of the wind and weather were effaced, until the great, square-set house was all as spick-and-span as though it had been erected yesterday. There were abundant signs that money was no consideration to General Heatherstone, and that it was not on the score of retrenchment that he had taken up his abode among us.

"It may be that he is devoted to study," suggested my father, as we discussed the question round the breakfast table. "Perhaps he has chosen this secluded spot to finish some *magnum opus* upon which he is engaged. If that is the case, I should be happy to let him have the run of my library."

Esther and I laughed at the grandiloquent manner in which he spoke of the two potato-sacks full of books.

"It may be as you say," said I, "but the general did not strike me during my short interview as being a man who was likely to have any very pronounced literary tastes. If I might hazard a guess, I should say that he is here upon medical advice, in the hopes that the complete quiet and fresh air may restore his shattered nervous system. If you had seen how he glared at me, and the twitching of his fingers, you would have thought it needed some restoring."

"I do wonder whether he has a wife and a family," said my sister. "Poor souls, how lonely they will be! Why, excepting ourselves, there is not a family that they could speak to for seven miles and more."

"General Heatherstone is a very distinguished soldier," remarked my father.

"Why, papa, however came you to know anything about him?"

"Ah, my dears," said my father, smiling at us over his coffee cup, "you were laughing at my library just now, but you see it may be very useful at times." As he spoke he took a red-covered volume from a shelf and turned over the pages. "This is an Indian Army List of three years back," he explained, "and here is the very gentleman we want—'Heatherstone, J. B., Commander of the Bath,' my dears, and 'V.C.', think of that, 'V.C.'—'formerly colonel in the Indian Infantry, 41st Bengal Foot, but now retired with the rank of major-general.' In this other column is a record of his services—'capture of Ghuznee and defense of Jellalabad, Sobraon 1848, Indian Mutiny and reduction of Oudh. Five times mentioned in dispatches.' I think, my dears, that we have cause to be proud of our new neighbor."

"It doesn't mention there whether he is married or not, I suppose," asked Esther.

"No," said my father, wagging his white head with a keen appreciation of his own humor. "It doesn't include that under the heading of 'daring actions'—thought it very well might, my dear, it very well might."

All our doubts, however, upon this head were very soon set at rest, for on the very day that the repairing and the furnishing had been completed I had occasion to ride into Wigtown, and I met upon the way a carriage which was bearing General Heatherstone and his family to their new home. An elderly lady, worn and sickly-looking was by his side, and opposite him sat a young fellow about my own age and a girl who appeared to be a couple of years younger. I raised my hat, and was about to pass them, when the general shouted to his coachman to pull up, and held out his hand to me. I could see now in the daylight that his face, although harsh and stern, was capable of assuming a not unkindly expression.

"How are you, Mr. Fothergill West?" he cried. "I must apologize to you if I was a little brusque the other night—you will excuse an old soldier who has spent the best part of his life in harness. All the same you must confess that you are rather darkskinned for a Scotchman."

"We have a Spanish strain in our blood," said I, wondering at his recurrence to the topic.

"That would of course account for it," he remarked. "My dear," to his wife, "allow me to introduce Mr. Fothergill West to you. This is my son and my daughter. We have come here in search of rest, Mr. West—complete rest."

"And you could not possibly have come to a better place," said I.

"Oh, you think so, he answered; "I suppose it is very quiet indeed, and very lonely. You might walk through these country lanes at night, I dare say, and never meet a soul, eh?"

"Well, there are not many about after dark," I said.

"And you are not much troubled with vagrants or wandering beggars, eh? Not many tinkers or tramps or rascally gypsies—no vermin of that sort about?"

"I find it rather cold," said Mrs. Heatherstone, drawing her thick sealskin mantle tighter round her figure. "We are detaining Mr. West, too."

"So we are, my dear, so we are. Drive on, coachman. Good day, Mr. West." The carriage rattled away towards the Hall, and I trotted thoughtfully onwards to the little country metropolis.

As I passed up the High Street Mr. McNeil ran out from his office and beckoned to me to stop. "Our new tenants have gone out," he said. "They drove over this morning."

"I met them on the way," I answered. As I looked down at the little factor I could see that his face was flushed and that he bore every appearance of having had an extra glass.

"Give me a real gentleman to do business with," he said, with a burst of laughter. "They understands me and I understands them. 'What shall I fill it up for?' says the general, taking a blank check out o' his pouch and laying it on the table. 'Two hundred,' says I, leaving a bit o' a margin for my own time and trouble."

"I thought that the landlord paid you for that," I remarked.

"Aye, aye, but it's well to have a bit margin. He filled it up and threw it over to me as if it had been an auld postage stamp. That's the way business should be done between honest men— though it wouldna' do if one was inclined to take an advantage. Will ye not come in, Mr. West, and have a taste of my whisky?"

"No, thank you," said I; "I have business to do."

"Well, well, business is the chief thing. It's well not to drink in the morning, too. For my own part, except a drop before breakfast to give me an appetite, and maybe a glass, or even twa, afterwards to promote digestion, I never touch spirits before noon. It may be that I'm over particular, but it's as well to be on the safe side. What d'ye think o' the general, Mr. West?"

"Why, I have hardly had an opportunity of judging," I answered.

Mr. McNeil tapped his forehead with his forefinger. "That's what I think of him," he said, in a confidential whisper. "He's gone, sir, in my estimation. Now what would you consider to be a proof of madness, Mr. West?"

"Why, offering a blank check to a Wigtown house-agent," said I.

"Ah, you're aye at your jokes. But between oorsels now, if a man asked ye how many miles it was frae a seaport, and whether ships come there from the East, and whether there were tramps on the road, and whether it was against the lease for him to build a high wall round the grounds, what would ye make of it, eh?"

"I should certainly think him eccentric," said I.

"If every man had his due, he would find himsel' in a house with a high wall round the grounds, and that without costing him a farthing," said the agent.

"Where then?" I asked.

"Why, in the Wigtown County Lunatic Asylum," cried the little man, with a bubble of laughter, in the midst of which I rode on my way, leaving him still chuckling over his own facetiousness.

The arrival of the new family at Cloomber Hall had no preceptible effect in relieving the monotony of our secluded district, for instead of entering into such simple pleasures as the country had to offer, or interesting themselves, as we had hoped, in our attempts to improve the lot of our poor crofters and fisher folk, they seemed to shun all observation, and hardly ever to venture beyond the avenue gates. We soon found too that the factor's words as to the inclosing of the grounds were founded upon fact, for gangs of workmen were kept hard at work from early in the morning until late at night in erecting a high wooden fence round the whole estate. When this was finished and topped with spikes Cloomber Park became impregnable to any one but an exceptionably daring climber. It was as if the old soldier had been so imbued with military ideas that, like my Uncle Toby, he could not refrain even in times of peace from standing upon the defensive. Stranger still, he had victualled the house as if for a siege, for Begbie, the chief grocer of Wigtown, told me himself that the general had sent him an order for hundreds of dozens of every imaginable potted meat and vegetable.

It may be imagined that all these incidents were not allowed to pass without comment. Over the whole country-side there was nothing but gossip about the new tenants of Cloomber Hall and the reasons which had led them to come among us. The only hypothesis, however, which the bucolic mind could evolve was that which had already occurred to Mr. McNeil, the factor—namely, that the old general and his family were one and all afflicted with madness, or, as an alternative conclusion, that he had committed some heinous offense and was endeavoring to escape the consequences of his misdeeds. These were both natural suppositions under the circumstances; but neither of them appeared to commend itself as a true explanation of the facts.

It is true that General Heatherstone's behavior on the occasion of our first interview was such as to suggest some suspicion of mental disease; but no man could have been more reasonable or more courteous than he had afterwards shown himself to be. Then, again, his wife and children led the same secluded life that he did himself; so that the reason could not be one peculiar to his own health. As to the possibility of his being a fugitive from justice, that theory was even more untenable. Wigtownshire was bleak and lonely, but it was not such an obscure corner of the world that a well-known soldier could hope to conceal himself there; nor would a man who feared publicity set every one's tongue wagging as the general had done. On the whole, I was inclined to believe that the true solution of the enigma lay in his own allusion to the love of quiet, and that they had taken shelter here with an almost morbid craving for solitude and repose. We very soon had an instance of the great lengths to which this desire for isolation would carry them.

My father had come down one morning with the weight of a great determination upon his brow. "You must put on your pink frock today, Esther," said he; "and you, John, you must make yourself smart, for I have determined that the three of us shall drive round this afternoon and pay our respects to Mrs. Heatherstone and the general."

"A visit to Cloomber!" cried Esther, clapping her hands.

"I am here," said my father, with dignity, "not only as the laird's agent, but also as his kinsman. In that capacity I am convinced that he would wish me to call upon these new comers and offer them any politeness which is in our power. At present they must feel lonely and friendless. What says the great Firdousi? 'The choicest ornaments to a man's house are his friends.'"

My sister and I knew by experience that when the old man began to justify his resolution by quotations from the Persian poets there was no chance of shaking it. Sure enough that afternoon saw the phaeton at the door, with my father perched upon the seat, with his second-best coat on and a pair of new driving-gloves.

"Jump in, my dears," he cried, cracking his whip briskly; "we shall show the general that he has no cause to be ashamed of his neighbors."

Alas, pride always goes before a fall! Our well-fed ponies and shining harness were not destined that day to impress the tenants of Cloomber with a sense of our importance. We had reached the avenue gate, and I was about to get out and open it, when our attention was arrested by a very large wooden placard, which was attached to one of the trees in such a manner that no one could possibly pass without seeing it. On the white surface of this board was printed in big, black letters the following hospitable inscriptions:—

GENERAL AND MRS. HEATHERSTONE
HAVE NO WISH
TO INCREASE
THE CIRCLE OF THEIR ACQUAINTANCE.

We all sat gazing at this announcement for some moments in silent astonishment. Then Esther and I, tickled by the absurdity of the thing, burst out laughing, but my father pulled the ponies' heads round, and drove home with compressed lips and the cloud of much wrath upon his brow. I have never seen the good man so thoroughly moved, and I am convinced that his anger did not arise from any petty feeling of injured vanity upon his own part, but from the thought that a slight had been offered to the Laird of Branksome, whose dignity he represented.

CHAPTER IV

OF A YOUNG MAN WITH A GREY HEAD

If I had any personal soreness on account of this family snub, it was a very passing emotion, and one which was soon effaced from my mind. It chanced that on the very next day after the episode I had occasion to pass that way and stopped to have another look at the obnoxious placard. I was standing staring up at it and wondering what could have induced our neighbor to take such an outrageous step, when I became suddenly aware of a sweet, girlish face which peeped out at me from between the bars of the gate, and of a white hand which eagerly beckoned me to approach. As I advanced to her I saw that it was the same young lady whom I had seen in the carriage.

"Mr. West," she said, in a quick whisper, glancing from side to side as she spoke in a nervous, hasty manner, "I wish to apologize to you for the indignity to which you and your family were subjected yesterday. My brother was in the avenue, and saw it all, but he is powerless to interfere. I assure you, Mr. West, that if that hateful thing," pointing up at the placard, "has given you any annoyance, it has given my brother and myself far more."

"Why, Miss Heatherstone?" said I, putting the matter off with a laugh. "Britain is a free country, and if a man chooses to warn off visitors from his premises there is no reason why he should not."

"It is nothing less than brutal," she broke out, with a petulant stamp of her foot. "To think that your sister, too, should have such an unprovoked insult offered to her! I am ready to sink with shame at the very thought."

"Pray do not give yourself one moment's uneasiness upon the subject," said I, earnestly, for I was grieved at her evident
19

distress. "I am sure that your father has some reason unknown to us for taking this step."

"God knows he has!" she answered, with ineffable sadness in her voice, "and yet I think it would be more manly to face a danger than to fly from it. However, he knows best, and it is impossible for us to judge. But who is this?" she exclaimed, anxiously peering up the dark avenue. "Oh, it is my brother Mordaunt. Mordaunt," she said, as the young man approached us, "I have been apologizing to Mr. West for what happened yesterday in your name as well as my own."

"I am very, very glad to have the opportunity of doing it in person," said he, courteously. "I only wish that I could see your sister and your father as well as yourself, to tell them how sorry I am. I think you had better run up to the house, little one, for it's getting near tiffin time. No—don't you go, Mr. West. I want to have a word with you."

Miss Heatherstone waved her hand to me with a bright smile, and tripped off up the avenue, while her brother unbolted the gate, and, passing through, closed it again, locking it upon the outside.

"I'll have a stroll down the road with you, if you have no objection. Have a manilla." He drew a couple of cheroots from his pocket and handed one to me. "You'll find they are not bad," he said. "I became a connoisseur in tobacco when I was in India. Are you lit? I hope I am not interfering with your business in coming along with you."

"Not at all," I answered. "I am very glad to have your company."

"I'll tell you a secret," said my companion. "This is the first time that I have been outside the grounds since we have been down here."

"And your sister?"

"She has never been out either," he answered. "I have given the governor the slip to-day, but he wouldn't half like it if he knew. It's a whim of his that we should keep ourselves entirely to ourselves. At least some people would call it a whim; for my own part I have reason to believe that he has solid grounds for all that he does—though perhaps in this matter he may be a little too exacting."

"You must surely find it very lonely," said I. "Couldn't you manage to slip down at times and have a smoke with me? That house over yonder is Branksome."

"Indeed you are very kind," he answered, with sparkling eyes. "I should dearly like to run over now and again. With the exception of Israel Stakes, our old coachman and gardener, I have not a soul that I can speak to."

"And your sister, she must feel it even more," said I, thinking in my heart that my new acquaintance made rather too much of his own troubles and too little of those of his companion.

"Yes; poor Gabriel feels it, no doubt," he answered, carelessly; "but it's a more unnatural thing for a young man of my age to be cooped up in this way than for a woman. Look at me now. I am three-and-twenty next March, and yet I have never been to a university, nor to a school, for that matter. I am as complete an ignoramus as any of these clodhoppers. It seems strange to you, no doubt; and yet it is so. Now, don't you think I deserve a better fate?" He stopped as he spoke, and faced round to me, throwing his palms forward in appeal.

As I looked at him, with the sun shining upon his face, he certainly did seem a strange bird to be cooped up in such a cage. Tall and muscular, with a keen, dark face, and sharp, finely-cut features, he might have stepped out of the canvas of Murillo or Velasquez. There was latent energy and power in his firm-set mouth, his square eyebrows, and the whole pose of his elastic, well-knit figure.

"There is the learning to be got from books and the learning to be got from experience," said I, sententiously. "If you have less of your share of the one, perhaps you have more of the other. I cannot believe that you have spent all your life in mere idleness and pleasure."

"Pleasure!" he cried. "Pleasure! Look at this." He pulled off his hat, and I saw that his black hair was all flecked and dashed with streaks of grey. "Do you imagine that this came from pleasure?" he asked, with a bitter laugh.

"You must have had some great shock," I said, astonished at the sight; "some terrible illness in your youth. Or perhaps it arises from a more chronic cause—a constant, gnawing anxiety. I have known men as young as you whose hair was as grey."

"Poor devils!" he muttered; "I pity them."

"If you can manage to slip down to Branksome at times," said I, "perhaps you could bring Miss Heatherstone with you. I know that my father and my sister would be delighted to see her, and a change, if only for an hour or two, might do her good."

"It would be rather hard for us both to get away together," he answered. "However, if I see a chance I shall bring her down. It might be managed some afternoon, perhaps, for the old man indulges in a siesta occasionally." We had reached the head of the winding lane which branches off from the high road and leads up to the laird's house, so my companion pulled up. "I must go back," he said, "or they will miss me. It's very kind of you, West, to take this interest in us. I'm very grateful to you, and so will Gabriel be when she hears of your kind invitation. It's a real heaping of coals of fire after that infernal placard of my father's."

He shook my hand and set off down the road, but he came running after me presently, calling me to stop. "I was just thinking," he said, "that you must consider us a great mystery up there at Cloomber. I dare say you have come to look upon it as a private lunatic asylum, and I can't blame you. If you are interested in the matter, I feel it is unfriendly upon my part not to satisfy your curiosity, but I have promised my father to be silent about it. And indeed, if I were to tell you all that I know you might not be very much the wiser after all. I would have you understand this, however—that my father is as sane as you or I, and that he has very good reasons for living the life which he does. I may add that his wish to remain secluded does not arise from any unworthy or dishonorable motives, but merely from the instinct of self-preservation."

"He is in danger, then!" I ejaculated.

"Yes; he is in constant danger."

"But why does he not apply to the magistrates for protection?" I asked. "If he is afraid of any one, he has only to name him and they will bind him over to keep the peace."

"My dear West," said young Heatherstone, "the danger with which my father is threatened is one that cannot be averted by any human intervention. It is none the less very real, and possibly very imminent."

"You don't mean to assert that it is supernatural," I said, incredulously.

"Well, hardly that, either," he answered with hesitation. "But there," he continued, "I have said rather more than I should, but I know that you will not abuse my confidence. Good-bye." He took to his heels and was soon out of my sight, round a curve in the country road.

A danger which was real and imminent, not to be averted by human means and yet hardly supernatural—here was a conundrum indeed! I had come to look upon the inhabitants of the Hall as mere eccentrics, but after what young Mordaunt Heatherstone had just told me, I could no longer doubt that some dark and sinister meaning underlay all their actions. The more I pondered over the problem, the more unanswerable did it appear, and yet I could not get the matter out of my thoughts. The lonely, isolated hall, and the strange, impending catastrophe which hung over its inmates, appealed forcibly to my imagination. All that evening, and late into the night, I sat moodily by the fire, pondering over all that I had heard, and revolving in my mind the various incidents which might furnish me with some clue to the mystery.

CHAPTER V

HOW FOUR OF US CAME TO BE UNDER THE
SHADOW OF CLOOMBER

I TRUST that my readers will not set me down as an inquisitive busybody when I say that as the days and weeks went by I found my attention and my thoughts more and more attracted to General Heatherstone and the mystery which surrounded him. It was in vain that I endeavored by hard work and strict attention to the laird's affairs to direct my mind into some more healthy channel. Do what I would, on land or on the water, I would still find myself puzzling over this one question, until it obtained such a hold upon me that I felt that it was useless for me to attempt to apply myself to anything until I had come to some satisfactory solution of it. I could never pass the dark line of five-foot fencing and the great iron gate, with its massive lock, without passing and racking my brain as to what the secret might be which was shut in by that inscrutable barrier. Yet with all my conjectures and all my observations I could never come to any conclusion which could for a moment be accepted as an explanation of the facts.

My sister had been out for a stroll one night, visiting a sick peasant, or performing some other of the numerous acts of charity by which she had made herself beloved by the whole countryside. "John," she said when she returned, "have you not observed Cloomber Hall at night?"

"No," I answered, laying down the book which I was reading. "Not since that memorable evening when the general and Mr. McNeil came over to make their inspection."

"Well, John, will you put your hat on and take a little walk with me?" I could see by her manner that something had agitated or frightened her.

"Why, bless the girl!" cried I, boisterously, "what is the matter? The old hall has not gone on fire, surely? You look as grave as if all Wigtown were in a blaze."

"Not quite so bad as that," she said, smiling. "But do come out, Jack. I should very much like you to see it."

I had always refrained from saying anything which might alarm my sister, so that she knew nothing of the interest which our neighbors' doings had for me. At her request I took my hat and followed her out into the darkness. She led the way along a little footpath over the moor, which brought us to some rising ground, from which we could look down upon the Hall without our view being obstructed by any of the fir-trees which had been planted round it. "Look at that," said my sister, pausing at the summit of this little eminence.

Cloomber lay beneath us in a blaze of light. In the lower floors the shutters obscured the illumination, but above, from the broad windows of the second story to the thin slits at the summit of the tower there was not a chink or an aperture which did not send forth a stream of radiance. So dazzling was the effect that for a moment I was persuaded that the house was on fire, but the steadiness and clearness of the light soon freed me from that apprehension. It was clearly the result of many lamps placed systematically all over the building. It added to the strange effect that all these brilliantly illuminated rooms were apparently untenanted, and some of them, as far as we could judge, were not even furnished. Through the whole great house there was no sign of movement or of life—nothing but the clear, unwinking flood of yellow light. I was still lost in wonder at the sight when I heard a short, quick sob at my side.

"What is it, Esther, dear?" I asked, looking down at my companion.

"I feel so frightened. Oh, John, John, take me home; I feel so frightened!" She clung to my arm, and pulled at my coat in a perfect frenzy of fear.

"It's all safe, darling," I said, soothingly. "There is nothing to fear. What has upset you so?"

"I am afraid of them, John; I am afraid of the Heatherstones. Why is their house lit up like this every night? I have heard from others that it is always so. And why does the old man run like a frightened hare if any one comes upon him. There is something wrong about it, John, and it frightens me."

I pacified her as well as I could, and led her home with me, where I took care that she should have some hot port negus before going to bed. I avoided the subject of the Heatherstones for fear of exciting her, and she did not recur to it of her own accord. I was convinced, however, from what I had heard from her that she had for some time back been making her own observations upon our neighbors, and that in doing so she had put a considerable strain upon her nerves. I could see that the mere fact of the Hall being illuminated at night was not enough to account for her extreme agitation, and that it must have derived its importance in her eyes from being one in a chain of incidents, all of which had left a weird or unpleasant impression upon her mind. That was the conclusion which I came to at the time, and I have reason to know not that I was right, and that my sister had even more cause than I had myself for believing that there was something uncanny about the tenants of Cloomber.

Our interest in the matter may have arisen at first from nothing higher than curiosity; but events soon took a turn which associated us more closely with the fortunes of the Heatherstone family. Mordaunt had taken advantage of my invitation to come down to the laird's house, and on several occasions he brought with him his beautiful sister. The four of us would wander over the moors together; or, perhaps, if the day were fine, set sail upon our little skiff and stand off into the Irish Sea. On such excursions the brother and sister would be as merry and as happy as two children. It was a keen pleasure to them to escape from their dull fortress, and to see, if only for a few hours, friendly and sympathetic faces round them. There could be but one result when four young people were brought together in sweet, forbidden intercourse. Acquaintanceship warmed into friendship, and friendship flamed suddenly into love. Gabriel sits beside me now as I write, and she agrees with me that, dear as is the subject to ourselves, the whole story of our mutual affection is of too personal a nature to be more than touched upon in this statement. Suffice it to say that, within a few weeks of our first meeting, Mordaunt Heatherstone had won the heart of my dear sister, and Gabriel had given me that pledge which death itself will not be able to break.

I have alluded in this brief way to the double tie which sprang up between the two families, because I have no wish that this narrative should degenerate into anything approaching to romance, or that I should lose the thread of the facts which I have set myself to chronicle. These are connected with General Heatherstone and only indirectly with my own personal history. It is enough if I say that after our engagement the visits to Branksome became more frequent, and that our friends were able sometimes to spend a whole day with us when business had called the general to Wigtown, or when his gout confined him to his room. As to our good father, he was ever ready to greet us with many small jests appropriate to the occasion; for we had no secrets from him, and he already looked upon us all as his children.

There were times when on account of some peculiarly dark or restless fit of the general's it was impossible for weeks on end for either Gabriel or Mordaunt to get away from the grounds. The old man would even stand on guard at the avenue gate, or pace up and down the drive as though he suspected that attempts had been made to penetrate his seclusion. Passing of an evening I have seen his dark, grim figure flitting about in the shadow of the trees, or caught a glimpse of his hard, angular face peering out at me from behind the bars. My heart would often sadden for him as I noticed his uncouth, nervous movements, his furtive glances and twitching features. Who would have believed that this slinking, covering creature had once been a dashing officer, who had fought the battles of his country and had won the palm of bravery among the host of brave men around him?

In spite of the old soldier's vigilance, we managed to hold communication with our friends. Immediately behind the Hall there was a spot where the fencing had been so carelessly erected that two of the rails could be removed without difficulty, leaving a broad gap, which gave us the opportunity for many a stolen interview, though they were necessarily short, for the general's movements were erratic, and no part of the grounds was secure from his visitations.

How vividly one of these hurried meetings rises before me! It stands out clear, peaceful and distinct amid the wild, mysterious incidents which were destined to lead up to the terrible catastrophe which has cast a shade over our lives. I can remember that as I walked through the fields the grass was damp with the rain of the morning, and the air was heavy with the smell of the fresh-turned earth. Gabriel was waiting for me under the hawthorn tree outside the gap, and we stood hand in hand looking down at the long sweep of moorland, and at the broad, blue channel which encircled it with its fringe of foam. Far away in the northwest the sun glinted upon the high peak of Mount Throston. From where we stood we could see the smoke of the steamers as they ploughed along the busy water-way which leads to Belfast.

"Is it not magnificent?" Gabriel cried, clasping her hands round my arm. "Ah, John, why are we not free to sail away over these waves together, and leave all our troubles behind us on the shore?"

"And what are the troubles which you would leave behind you, dear one?" I asked. "May I not know them, and help you to bear them?"

"I have no secrets from you, John," she answered. "Our chief trouble is, as you may guess, our poor father's strange behavior. Is it not a sad thing for all of us that a man who has played such a distinguished part in the world should skulk from one obscure corner of the country to another, and should defend himself with locks and barriers as though he were a common thief flying from justice? This is a trouble, John, which it is out of your power to alleviate."

"But why does he do it, Gabriel?" I asked.

"I cannot tell," she answered frankly. "I know only that he imagines some deadly danger to be hanging over his head, and that this danger was incurred by him during his stay in India. What its nature may be I have no more idea than you have."

"Then your brother has," I remarked. "I am sure from the way in which he spoke to me about it one day that he knows what it is, and that he looks upon it as real."

"Yes, he knows, and so does my mother," she answered; "but they have always kept it secret from me. My poor father is very excited at present. Day and night he is in an agony of apprehension, but it will soon be the 5th of October, and after that he will be at peace."

"How do you know that?" I asked in surprise.

"By experience," said she, gravely. "On the fifth of October these fears of his come to a crisis. For years back he has been in the habit of locking Mordaunt and myself up in our rooms on that date, so that we have no idea what occurs; but we have always found that he has been much relieved afterwards, and has continued to be comparatively in peace until that day began to draw round again."

"Then you have only ten days or so to wait," I remarked, for September is drawing to a close. "By the way, dearest, why is it that you light up all your rooms at night?"

"You have noticed it, then?" she said. It comes also from my father's fears. He does not like to have one dark corner in the whole house. He walks about a good deal at night, and inspects everything, from the attics right down to the cellars. He has large lamps in every room and corridor, even the empty ones, and he orders the servants to light them all at dusk."

"I am rather surprised that you manage to keep your servants," I said, laughing. "The maids in these parts are a superstitious class, and their imaginations are easily excited by anything which they don't understand."

"The cook and both housemaids are from London, and are used to our ways. We pay them on a very high scale to make up for any inconvenience to which they may be put. Israel Stakes, the coachman, is the only one who comes from this part of the country, and he seems to be a stolid, honest fellow, who is not easily scared."

"Poor little girl," I exclaimed, looking down at the slim, graceful figure by my side. "This is no atmosphere for you to live in. Why will you not let me rescue you from it? Why won't you allow me to go straight and ask the general for your hand? At the worst he could only refuse."

She turned quite haggard and pale at the very thought. "For God's sake, John," she cried, earnestly, "do nothing of the kind. He would whip us all away in the dead of the night, and within a week we should be settling down again in some wilderness where we might never have a chance of seeing or hearing from you again. Besides, he never would forgive us for venturing out of the grounds."

"I don't think that he is a hard-hearted man," I remarked. "I have seen a kindly look in his eyes, for all his stern face."

"He can be the kindest of fathers," she answered. "But he is terrible when opposed or thwarted. You have never seen him so, and I trust you never will. It was that strength of will and impatience of opposition which made him such a splendid officer. I assure you that in India every one thought a great deal of him. The soldiers were afraid of him, but they would have followed him anywhere."

"And had he these nervous attacks then?"

"Occasionally; but not nearly so acutely. He seems to think that the danger—whatever it may be—becomes more imminent every year. Oh, John, it is terrible to be waiting like this with a sword over our heads—and all the more terrible to me since I have no idea where the blow is to come from."

"Dear Gabriel," I said, taking her hand and drawing her to my side, "look over all this pleasant country-side and the broad, blue sea. Is it not all peaceful and beautiful? In these cottages with their red-tiled roofs peeping out from the grey moor, there live none but simple, God-fearing men, who toil hard at their crofts and bear enmity to no man. Within seven miles of us is a large town, with every civilized appliance for the preservation of order. Ten miles further there is a garrison quartered, and a telegram would at any time bring down a company of soldiers. Now, I ask you, dear, in the name of common sense, what conceivable danger could threaten you in this secluded neighborhood with the means of help so near? You assure me that the peril is not connected with your father's health?"

"No, I am sure of that. It is true that Dr. Easterling, of Stranraer, has been over to see him once or twice, but that was merely for some small indisposition. I can assure you that the danger is not to be looked for in that direction."

"Then I can assure *you*," said I, laughing, "that there is no danger at all. It must be some strange monomania or hallucination. No other hypothesis will cover the facts."

"Would my father's monomania account for the fact of my brother's hair being turned grey and my mother wasting away to a mere shadow?"

"Undoubtedly," I answered. "The long-continued worry of the general's restlessness and irritability would produce those effects on sensitive natures."

"No, no," said she, shaking her head sadly; "I have been exposed to his restlessness and irritability, but they have had no such effect upon me. The difference between us lies in the fact that they know this awful secret and we do not."

"My dear girl," said I, "the days of family apparitions and that kind of thing are gone. Nobody is haunted nowadays, so we can put that supposition out of the question. Having done so, what remains? There is absolutely no other theory which could even be suggested. Believe me, the whole mystery is that the heat of India has been too much for your poor father's brain."

What she would have answered I cannot tell, for at that moment she gave a start as if some sound had fallen upon her ear. As she looked round apprehensively I suddenly saw her features become rigid and her eyes fixed and dilated. Following the direction of her gaze, I felt a sudden thrill of fear pass through me as I perceived a human face surveying us from behind one of the trees—a face every feature of which was distorted by the most malignant hatred and anger. Finding himself observed he stepped out and advanced towards us, when I saw it was none other than the general himself. His beard was all a-bristle with fury, and his deep-set eyes glowed from under their heavily-veined lids with a most sinister and demoniacal brightness.

CHAPTER VI

HOW I CAME TO BE ENLISTED AS ONE OF THE
GARRISON OF CLOOMBER

"To your room, girl!" he cried in a hoarse, harsh voice, stepping in between us and pointing authoritatively towards the house. He waited until Gabriel, with a last frightened glance at me, had passed through the gap, and then he turned upon me with an expression so murderous that I stepped back a pace or two, and tightened my grasp upon my oak stick.

"You—you—" he sputtered, with his hand up to his throat, as though his fury were choking him. "You have dared to intrude upon my privacy! Do you think I built this fence that all the vermin in the country might congregate round it! Oh, you have been very near your death, my fine fellow! You will never be nearer until your time comes. Look at this!" He pulled a squat, thick pistol out of his bosom. "If you had passed through that gap and set foot on my land I'd have let daylight into you. I'll have no vagabonds here! I know how to treat gentry of that sort, whether their faces are black or white.

"Sir," said I, "I meant no harm by coming here, and I do not know how I have deserved this extraordinary outburst. Allow me to observe, however, that you are still covering me with your pistol, and that, as your hand is rather tremulous, it is more than possible that it may go off. If you don't turn the muzzle down I shall be compelled in self-defence to strike you over the wrist with my stick."

"What the devil brought you here, then?" he asked, in a more composed voice, putting his weapon back into his bosom. "Can't a gentleman live quietly without your coming to peep and pry? Have you no business of your own to look after, eh? And my

33

daughter? how came you to know anything of her? and what have you been trying to squeeze out of her? It wasn't chance that brought you here."

"No," said I, boldly, "it was not chance which brought me here. I have had several opportunities of seeing your daughter and of appreciating her many noble qualities. We are engaged to be married to each other, and I came up with the express intention of seeing her."

Instead of blazing into a fury, as I had expected, the general gave a long whistle of astonishment, and then leaned up against the railings, laughing softly to himself.

"English terriers are fond of playing with worms," he remarked at last. "When we used to bring them out to India they used to trot off into the jungle and begin sniffing at what they imagined to be worms there. But the worm turned out to be a venomous snake, and so poor doggy paid the penalty. I think you'll find yourself in a somewhat analogous position if you don't look out."

"You surely don't mean to cast an aspersion upon your own daughter?" I said, flushing with indignation.

"Oh, Gabriel is all right," he answered, carelessly. "Our family is not exactly one, however, which I should recommend a young fellow to marry into. And pray how is it that I was not informed of this snug little arrangement of yours?"

"We were afraid, sir, that you might separate us," I replied, feeling that perfect candor was the best policy under the circumstances. "It is possible that we were mistaken. Before coming to any final decision I implore you to remember that the happiness of both of us is at stake. It is in your power to divide our bodies, but our souls shall be forever united."

"My good fellow," said the general, in a not unkindly tone, "you don't know what you are asking for. There is a gulf between you and any one of the blood of Heatherstone which can never be bridged over." All trace of anger had vanished now from his manner, and given place to an air of somewhat contemptuous amusement.

My family pride took fire at his words. "The gulf may be less than you imagine," I said, coldly. "We are not clodhoppers because we live in this out-of-the-way place. I am of noble descent on one side, and my mother was a Buchan of Buchan. I assure you that there is no such disparity between us as you seem to imagine."

"You misunderstand me," the general answered. "It is on our side that the disparity lies. There are reasons why my daughter Gabriel should live and die single. It would not be to your advantage to marry her."

"But surely, sir," I persisted, "I am the best judge of my own interests and advantages. Since you take this ground all becomes easy; for I do assure you that the one interest which overrides all others is that I should have the woman I love for my wife. If this is your only objection to our match, you may surely give us your consent, for any danger or trial which I may incur in marrying Gabriel will not weigh with me one featherweight."

"Here's a young bantam!" exclaimed the old soldier, smiling at my warmth. "It's easy to defy danger when you don't know what the danger is."

"What is it, then?" I asked, hotly. "There is no earthly peril that will drive me from Gabriel's side. Let me know what it is and test me."

"No, no. That would never do," he answered with a sigh; and then, thoughtfully, as if speaking his mind aloud: "He has plenty of pluck, and is a well-grown lad, too. We might do worse than make use of him." He went on mumbling to himself with a vacant stare in his eyes as if he had forgotten my presence.

"Look, here, West," he said, presently. "You'll excuse me if I spoke hastily a little time ago. It is the second time that I have had occasion to apologize to you for the same offense. It shan't occur again. I am rather over-particular, no doubt, in my desire for complete isolation; but I have good reasons for insisting on the point. Rightly or wrongly, I have got it into my head that some day there might be an organized raid upon my grounds. If anything of the sort should occur I suppose I might reckon upon your assistance?"

"With all my heart."

"So that if ever you got a message such as 'Come up,' or even simply 'Cloomber!' you would know that it was an appeal for help and would hurry up immediately, even if it were in the dead of the night?"

"Most certainly I should," I answered. "But might I ask you what the nature of the danger is which you apprehend?"

"There would be nothing gained by your knowing. Indeed, you would hardly understand it if I told you. I must bid you good-day now, for I have stayed with you too long. Remember, I count upon you as one of the Cloomber garrison now."

"One other thing, sir," I said, hurriedly, for he was turning away; "I hope that you will not be angry with your daughter for anything which I have told you. It was for my sake that she kept it all secret from you."

"All right," he said, with his cold, inscrutable smile. "I am not such an ogre in the bosom of my family as you seem to think. As to this marriage question, I should advise you as a friend to let it drop altogether, but if that is impossible I must insist that it stand over completely for the present. It is impossible to say what unexpected turn events may take. Goodbye!" He plunged into the wood and was quickly out of sight among the dense plantation.

Thus ended this extraordinary interview, in which this strange man had begun by pointing a loaded pistol at my breast and had ended by partially acknowledging the possibility of my becoming his future son-in-law. I hardly knew whether to be cast down or elated over it. On the one hand, he was likely, by keeping a closer watch over his daughter, to prevent us from communicating as freely as we had done hitherto. Against this there was the advantage of having obtained an implied consent to the renewal of my suit at some future date. On the whole, I came to the conclusion, as I walked thoughtfully home, that I had improved my position by the incident.

But this danger—this shadowy, unspeakable danger—which appeared to rise up at every turn, and to hang day and night over the towers of Cloomber! Rack my brain as I would I could not conjure up any solution to the problem which was not puerile and inadequate. One fact struck me as being significant. Both the father and the son had assured me, independently of each other, that if I were told what the peril was, I would hardly realize its significance. How strange and bizarre must the fear be which can scarce be expressed in intelligible language. I held up my hand in the darkness before I turned to sleep that night, and I swore that no power of man or devil should ever weaken my love for the woman whose pure heart I had had the good fortune to win.

CHAPTER VII

OF CORPORAL RUFUS SMITH AND
HIS COMING TO CLOOMBER

In making this statement I have purposely couched it in bald and simple language, for fear I should be accused of coloring my narrative for the sake of effect. If, however, I have told my story with any approach to realism, the reader will understand me when I say that by this time the succession of dramatic incidents which had occurred had arrested my attention and excited my imagination to the exclusion of all minor topics. How could I plod through the dull routine of an agent's work, or interest myself in the thatch of this tenant's bothy or the sails of that one's boat, when my mind was taken up by the chain of events which I have described, and was still busy seeking an explanation for them? Go where I would over the country-side I could see the square, white tower shooting out from among the trees, and beneath that tower this ill-fated family were watching and waiting, waiting and watching—and for what? That was still the question which stood like an impassable barrier at the end of every train of thought. Regarded merely as an abstract problem, this mystery of the Heatherstone family had a lurid fascination about it, but when the woman whom I loved a thousandfold better than I did myself proved to be so deeply interested in the solution, I felt that it was impossible to turn my thoughts to anything else until it had been finally cleared up.

My good father had received a letter from the laird, dated from Naples, which told us that he had derived much benefit from the change, and that he had no intention of returning to Scotland for some time. This was satisfactory to all of us, for my father had found Branksome such an excellent place for study that it would have been a sore trial to him to return to the noise and tumult of a city. As to my dear sister and myself, there were, as I have shown, stronger reasons still to make us love the Wig-townshire moors.

In spite of my interview with the general—or perhaps I might say on account of it—I took occasion at least twice a day to walk towards Cloomber and satisfy myself that all was well there. He had begun by resenting my intrusion, but he had ended by tak-ing me into a sort of half confidence, and even by asking my assistance, so I felt that I stood upon a different footing with him than I had done formerly, and that he was less likely to be an-noyed by my presence. Indeed, I met him pacing round the inclosure a few days afterwards, and his manner towards me was civil, though he made no allusion to our former conversation. He appeared to be still in an extreme state of nervousness, start-ing from time to time, and gazing furtively about him. I hoped that his daughter was right in naming the fifth of October as the turning-point of his complaint, for it was evident to me, as I looked at his gleaming eyes and quivering hands, that a man could not live long in such a state of nervous tension.

I found on examination that he had had the loose rails se-curely fastened so as to block up our former trysting-place, and though I prowled round the whole long line of fencing, I was unable to find any other place where an entrance could be ef-fected. Here and there between chinks of the barrier I could catch glimpses of the Hall, and once I saw a rough-looking, middle-aged man standing at a window at the lower floor, whom I supposed to be Israel Stakes, the coachman. There was no sign, however, of Gabriel or of Mordaunt, and their absence alarmed me. I was convinced that, unless they were under some restraint, they would have managed to communicate with my sister or myself. My fears became more and more acute as day followed day without our seeing or hearing anything of them.

One morning—it was the second day of October—I was walking towards the Hall, hoping that I might be fortunate enough to learn some news of my darling, when I observed a man perched upon a stone at the side of the road. As I came nearer to him I could see that he was a stranger, and from his dusty clothes and dilapidated appearance he seemed to have come from a distance. He had a great hunch of bread on his knee and a clasp knife in his hand, but he had apparently just finished his breakfast, for he brushed the crumbs off his lap and rose to his feet when he perceived me. Noticing the great height of the fellow, and that he still held his weapon, I kept well to the other side of the road, for I knew that destitution makes men desperate and that the chain which glittered on my waistcoat might be too great a temptation to him upon this lonely highway. I was confirmed in my fears when I saw him step out into the centre of the road and bar my progress.

"Well, my lad," I said, affecting an ease which I by no means felt, "what can I do for you this morning?"

The fellow's face was the color of mahogany with exposure to the weather, and he had a deep scar from the corner of his mouth to his ear, which by no means improved his appearance. His hair was grizzled, but his figure was stalwart, and his fur cap was cocked on one side so as to give him a rakish, semi-military appearance. Altogether, he gave me the impression of being one of the most dangerous types of tramp that I had ever fallen in with.

Instead of replying to my question he eyed me for some time in silence, with sullen, yellow-shot eyes, and then closed his knife with a loud snick. "You're not a beak," he said; "too young for that, I guess. They had me in chokey at Paisley, and they had me in chokey at Wigtown, but by the living thunder if another of them lays a hand on me I'll make him remember Corporal Rufus Smith! It's a darned fine country this, where they won't give a man work and then lay him by the heels for having no visible means of subsistence."

"I am sorry to see an old soldier so reduced," said I. "What corps did you serve in?"

"H Battery, Royal Horse Artillery. Bad cess to the service and every one in it! Here I am nigh sixty years of age, with a beggarly pension of thirty-eight pound ten—not enough to keep me in beer and baccy."

"I should have thought thirty-eight pound ten a year would have been a nice help to you in your old age," I remarked.

"Would you though?" he answered with a sneer, pushing his weather-beaten face forward until it was within a foot of my own. "How much d'ye think that slash with a tulwar is worth? and my foot with the bones rattling about like a bagful of dice? What's that worth, eh? And a liver like a sponge, and ague whenever the wind comes round to the east—what's the market value of that? Would you take the lot for a dirty forty pound a year—would you now?"

"We are poor folk in this part of the country," I answered. "You would pass for a rich man down here."

"They are simple folk and they have simple tastes," and he, drawing a black pipe from his pocket and stuffing it with tobacco. "I know what good living is, and while I have a shilling in my pocket I like to spend it as a shilling should be spent. I've fought for my country, and my country has done darned little for me. I'll go to the Rooshians, so help me! I could show them how to cross the Himalayas, so that it would puzzle either Afghans or British to stop 'em. What's that secret worth in St. Petersburg, I wonder!"

"I'm ashamed to hear an old soldier speak so, even in jest," said I sternly.

"Jest, indeed!" he cried, with a great oath. "I'd have done it years ago, if the Rooshians had been game to take it up. Skobeloff was the best of the bunch, but he's been snuffed out. However, that's neither here nor there. What I want to ask you is whether you've ever heard anything in this quarter of a man called Heatherstone, the same who used to be colonel of the 41st Bengaless? They told me at Wigtown that he lived somewhere down this way."

"He lives in that large house over there," said I, pointing to Cloomber Tower. "You'll find the avenue gate a little way down the road, but the general isn't over fond of visitors."

The last part of my speech was lost upon Corporal Rufus Smith; for the instant that I pointed out the gate he set off hopping down the road. His mode of progression was the most singular which I have ever seen, for he would only put his right foot to the ground once in every half-dozen strides, while he worked so hard and attained such a momentum with the other limb that he got over the ground at an astonishing speed. I was so surprised that I stood in the roadway gazing after his hulking figure until the thought suddenly struck me that some serious result might come from a meeting between a man of such blunt speech and the choleric hot-headed general. I therefore followed him as he hopped along like some great, clumsy bird, and overtook him at the avenue gate, where he stood grasping the ironwork and peering through at the dark carriage drive beyond.

"He's a sly old fox," he said, looking round at me and nodding his head in the direction of the Hall. "He's a deep old dog. And that's his bungalow, is it, among the trees?"

"That is his house," I answered; "but I should advise you to keep a more civil tongue in your head if you intend to speak with the general. He is not a man to stand any nonsense."

"Right you are. He was always a hard nut to crack. But isn't this him coming down the avenue?"

I looked through the gate and saw that it was indeed the general, who having either seen us or been attracted by our voices, was hurrying down towards us. As he advanced he would stop from time to time and peer at us through the dark shadow thrown by the trees, as if he were irresolute whether to come on or no.

"He's reconnoitering!" whispered my companion with a hoarse chuckle. "He's afraid—and I know what he's afraid of. He won't be caught in a trap if he can help it, the old un! He's about as fly as they make 'em, you bet!" Then suddenly standing on his tiptoes and waving his hand through the bars of the gate, he shouted at the top of his voice, "Come on, my gallant commandant! Come on! The coast's clear, and no enemy in sight."

This familiar address had the effect of reassuring the general, for he came right for us, though I could tell by his heightened color that his temper was at boiling point. "What, you here, Mr. West?" he said, as his eye fell upon me. "What is it you want, and why have you brought this fellow with you?"

"I have not brought him with me, sir," I answered, feeling rather disgusted at being made responsible for the presence of the disreputable-looking vagabond beside me. "I found him on the road here, and he desired to be directed to you, so I showed him the way. I know nothing of him myself."

"What do you want with me, then?" the general asked sternly, turning to my companion.

"If you please, sir," said the ex-corporal, speaking in a whining voice, and touching his moleskin cap with a humility which contrasted strangely with the previous rough independence of his bearing, "I am an old gunner in the Queen's service, sir, and knowing your name by hearing it in India I thought that maybe you would take me as your groom or gardener, or give me any other place as happened to be vacant."

"I am sorry that I cannot do anything for you, my man," the old soldier answered, impassively.

"Then you'll give me a little just to help me on my way, sir," said the cringing mendicant. "You won't see an old comrade go to the bad for the sake of a few rupees. I was with Sale's brigade in the Passes, sir, and I was at the second taking of Cabul."

General Heatherstone looked keenly at the supplicant, but was silent to his appeal.

"I was in Ghuznee with you when the walls were all shook down by an earthquake, and when we found forty thousand Afghans within gunshot of us. You ask me about it, and you'll see whether I'm lying or not. We went through all this when we were young, and now that we are old you are to live in a fine bungalow, and I am to starve by the roadside. It don't seem to me to be fair."

"You are an impertinent scoundrel," said the general. "If you had been a good soldier you would never need to ask for help. I shall not give you a farthing."

"One word more, sir," cried the tramp, for the other was turning away; "I've been in the Tarada Pass."

The old soldier sprang round as if the words had been a pistol-shot. "What—what d'ye mean?" he stammered.

"I've been in the Tarada Pass, sir, and I knew a man there called Ghoolab Shah."

These last words were hissed out in an undertone, and a malicious grin overspread the face of the speaker.

Their effect upon the general was extraordinary. He fairly staggered back from the gateway, and his yellow countenance blanched to a livid, mottled grey. For a moment he was too overcome to speak. At last he gasped out, "Ghoolab Shah!—who are you who know Ghoolab Shah?"

"Take another look," said the tramp; "your sight is not as keen as it was forty years ago."

The general took a long, earnest look at the unkempt wanderer in front of him, and as he gazed I saw the light of recognition spring up in his eyes. "God bless my soul!" he cried. "Why, it's Corporal Rufus Smith."

"You've come on it at last," said the other, chuckling to himself. "I was wondering how long it would be before you knew me. And first of all just unlock this gate, will you? It's hard to talk through a grating. It's too much like ten minutes with a visitor in the cells."

The general, whose face still bore evidences of his agitation, undid the bolts with nervous, trembling fingers. The recognition of Corporal Rufus Smith had, I fancied, been a relief to him, and yet he plainly showed by his manner that he regarded his presence as by no means an unmixed blessing.

"Why, corporal," he said, as the gate swung open, "I have often wondered whether you were dead or alive, but I never expected to see you again. How have you been all these long years?"

"How have I been?" the corporal answered gruffly. "Why I have been drunk for the most part. When I draw my money I lay it out in liquor, and as long as that lasts I get some peace in life. When I'm cleaned out I go upon a tramp, partly in the hope of picking up the price of a dram, and partly in order to look for you."

"You'll excuse us talking about these private matters, West," the general said, looking round at me, for I was beginning to move away. "Don't leave us. You know something of this matter already, and may find yourself entirely in the swim with us some of these days."

Corporal Rufus Smith looked round at me in blank astonishment. "In the swim with us!" he said. "However did he get there?"

"Voluntarily, voluntarily," the general explained, hurriedly sinking his voice. "He is a neighbor of mine, and he has volunteered his help in case I should ever need it."

This explanation seemed, if anything, to increase the big stranger's surprise. "Well, if that don't lick cock-fighting!" he exclaimed, contemplating me with admiration. "I never heard tell of such a thing."

"And now that you have found me, Corporal Smith," said the tenant of Cloomber, "what is it that you want of me?"

"Why, everything; I want a roof to cover me, and clothes to wear, and food to eat, and above all, brandy to drink."

"Well, I'll take you in and do what I can for you," said the general, slowly. "But look here, Smith, we must have discipline. I'm the general and you are the corporal; I am the master and you are the man. Now don't let me have to remind you of that again."

The tramp drew himself up to his full height and raised his right hand with the palm forward in a military salute.

"I can take you on as gardener and get rid of the fellow I have got. As to brandy, you shall have an allowance and no more. We are not deep drinkers at the Hall."

"Don't you take opium, or brandy, or nothing yourself, sir?" asked Corporal Rufus Smith.

"Nothing," the general said, firmly.

"Well, all I can say is, that you've got more nerve and pluck than I shall ever have. I don't wonder now at your winning that cross in the Mutiny. If I was to go on listening night after night to them things without ever taking a drop of something to cheer my heart—why, it would above drive me silly."

General Heatherstone put his hand up, as though afraid that his companion might say too much. "I must thank you, Mr. West," he said, "for having shown this man my door. I would not willingly allow an old comrade, however humble, to go to the bad, and if I did not acknowledge his claim more readily it was simply because I had my doubts as to whether he was really what he represented himself. Just walk up to the Hall, corporal, and I shall follow you in a minute."

"Poor devil!" he continued, as he watched the new-comer hobbling up the avenue in the ungainly manner which I have described. "He got a 64-pound shot on his foot, and it crushed the bones, but the obstinate fool would not let the doctors take it off. I remember him now as a smart young soldier in Afghanistan. He and I were associated in some queer adventures, which I may tell you of some day, and I naturally feel sympathy towards him, and would befriend him. Did he tell you anything about me before I came?"

"Not a word," I replied.

"Oh," said the general, carelessly, but with an evident expression of relief. "I thought perhaps he might have said something of old times. Well, I must go and look after him, or the servants will be frightened, for he isn't a beauty to look at. Good-bye!" With a wave of the hand the old man turned away from me and hurried up the drive after this unexpected addition to his household, while I strolled on round the high black paling, peering through every chink between the planks, but without seeing a trace either of Mordaunt or of his sister.

I have now brought this statement down to the coming of Corporal Rufus Smith, which will prove to be the beginning of the end. I have set down soberly and in order the events which brought us to Wigtownshire, the arrival of the Heatherstones at Cloomber, and many strange incidents which excited first our curiosity and finally our intense interest in that family, and I have briefly touched upon the circumstances which brought my sister and myself into a closer and more personal relationship with them. I think that there cannot be a better moment than this to hand the narrative over to those who had means of knowing something of what was going on inside Cloomber during the months that I was observing it from without. The evidence of the two individuals whose statements I shall now lay before the reader, does not, it is true, amount to very much, but there are a few notable facts contained in it, and it corroborates and amplifies my own experience. Israel Stakes, the coachman, proved to be unable to read or write, but Mr. Mathew Clark, the Presbyterian minister at Stoneykirk, has copied down his deposition, duly attested by the cross set opposite his name. The good clergyman has, I fancy, put some slight polish upon the narrator's story, which I rather regret, as it might have been more interesting, if less intelligible, when reported verbatim. It still preserves, however, considerable traces of Israel's individuality, and may be regarded as an exact record of what he saw and did while in General Heatherstone's service.

CHAPTER VIII

STATEMENT OF ISRAEL STAKES

[*Copied and authenticated by the Reverend Mathew Clark, Presbyterian minister of Stoneykirk, in Wigtownshire.*]

MAISTER FOTHERGILL WEST and the meenister say that I maun tell all I can aboot General Heatherstone and his hoose, but that I maunna' say muckle aboot mysel' because the readers wouldna' care to hear aboot me or my affairs. I am na sae sure o' that, for the Stakes is a family weel kenned and respecked on baith sides o' the border, and there's mony in Nithsdale and Annendale as would be gey pleased to hear news o' the son o' Archie Stakes, o' Ecclefechan. I maun e'en do as I'm tauld, however, for Mr. West's sake, hoping he'll no forget me when I chance to hae a favor tae ask.* I am no able tae write mysel' because my feyther sent me oot to scare craws instead o' sendin' me tae school, but on the ither hond he brought me up in the preenciples and practise o' the real kirk o' the Covenant, for which may the Lord be praised!

It was last May twel'month that the factor body, Maister McNeil, cam' ower tae me in the street and speered whether I was in want o' a place as a coachman and gaird'ner. As it fell oot I chanced tae be on the look oot for something o' the sort mysel' at the time, but I wasna' ower quick to let him see that I wanted it.

"Ye can tak' it or leave it," says he sharp-like. "It's a guid place, and there's many would be glad o't. If ye want it ye can come up tae my office at twa the morn and put your ain questions tae the gentleman."

*The old rascal was well paid for his trouble, so he need not have made such a favor of it.—J. F. W.

49

That was a' I could get frae him, for he's a close man and a hard one at a bargain—which shall profit him leetle in the next life, though he lay by a store o' siller in this. When the day comes there'll be a hantle o' factors on the left hand o' the throne and I shouldna' be surprised if Maister McNeil found himsel' amang them.

"Well, on the morn I gaed up to the office and there I foond the factor and a lang, thin, dour man wi' grey hair and a face as brown and crinkled as a walnut. He looked hard at me wi' a pair o' e'en that glowed like twa spunks, and then he says, says he;

"You've been born in these parts, I understan'?"

"Aye," says I, "and never left them, neither."

"Never been oot o' Scotland?" he speers.

"Twice to Carlisle fair," says I, for I am a man wha loves the truth; and besides I kenned that the factor would mind my gaeing there, for I bargained for twa steers and a stirk that he wanted for the stockin' o' the Drumcleugh Fairm.

"I learn frae Maister McNeil," says General Heatherstone—for him it was and nane ither, "that ye canna' write."

"Na," says I.

"Nor read?"

"Na," says I.

"It seems tae me," says he, turnin' tae the factor, "that this is the vera man I want. Servants is spoiled noo-a-days," says he, "by ower muckle eddication. I have nae doobt, Stakes, that ye will suit me well eneugh. Ye'll hae three pund a month and a' foond, but I shall resairve the right o' givin' ye twenty-four hoors' notice at any time. How will that suit ye?"

"It's vera different frae my last place," says I, discontented-like. And the words were true eneugh, for auld Fairmer Scott only gave me a pund a month and parritch twice a day.

"Weel, weel," says he, "maybe we'll gie ye a rise if ye suit. Meanwhile here's the hansel shillin' that Maister McNeil tells me it's the custom tae give, and I shall expec' tae see ye at Cloomber on Monday."

When the Monday cam' roond I walked oot tae Cloomber, and a great muckle hoose it is wi' a hundred windows or mair, and space enough tae hide awa' half the parish. As tae gairden-

ing there was no gairden for me tae work at, and the horse was
never taken oot o' the stables frae week's end tae week's end. I
was busy eneugh for a' that, for there was a deal o' fencing tae
be put up and one thing or anither, forbye cleanin' the knives
and brushin' the boots and such-like jobs as is mair fit for an
auld wife than for a grown man. There was twa beside mysel' in
the kitchen, the cook Eliza, and Mary the hoosemaid, puir, be-
nighted things, baith o' them, wha had wasted a' their lives in
Lunnon, and kenned leetle aboot the warld or the ways o' the
flesh, I hadna' muckle tae say to them for they were simple folk
wha could scarce understand English, and had hardly mair regard for their ain souls than the tods on the moor. When the
cook said she didna' think muckle o' John Knox, and the ither
that she wouldn't gie saxpence tae hear the discourse o' Maister
Donald McSnaw o' the true kirk, I kenned it was time for me
tae leave them tae a higher Judge.

There was four in family, the general, my leddy, Maister
Mordaunt and Miss Gabriel, and it wasna' lang before I found
that a' wasna' just exactly as it should be. My leddy was as thin
and as white as a ghaist, and many's the time as I've come on her
and found her yammerin' and greetin' all by hersel'. I've
watched her walkin' up and doon in the wood where she thought
nane could see her and wringin' her honds like one demented.
There was the young gentleman tae and his sister—they baith
seemed to hae some trouble on their minds, and the general
maist of a', for the ithers were up ane day and down anither; but
he was aye the same, wi' a face as dour and sad as a felon when
he feels the tow roond his neck.

I speered o' the hussies in the kitchen whether they kenned
what was amiss wi' the family, but the cook she answered me
back that it wasna' for her tae inquire into the affairs o' her superiors and that it was naething to her as long as she did her
work and had her wages. They were puir, feckless bodies, the
twa o' them, and would scarce gie an answer tae a ceevil question though they could clack loud eneugh when they had a
mind.

Weel, weeks passed into months and a' things grew waur instead o' better in the Hall. The general he got mair nairvous,

and his leddy mair melancholy every day, and yet there wasna' any quarrel or bickering between them, for when they've been together in the breakfast room I used often tae gang round and prune the rose tree alongside o' the window, so that I couldna' help hearin' a great pairt o' their conversation, though sair against the grain. When the young folk were wi' them they would speak little, but when they had gone they would aye talk as if some waefu' trial were aboot to fa' upon them, though I could never gather from their words what it was that they were afeard o'. I've heard the general say mair than ance that he wasna' frighted o' death, or of any danger that he could face and have done wi', but that it was the lang, weary waitin' and the uncertainty that had taken a' the strength and the mettle oot o' him. Then my leddy would console him and tell him that maybe it wasna' as bad as he thought and that a' would come richt in the end—but a' her cheery words were clean throwed away upon him. As tae the young folk I kenned weel that they dinna' bide in the groonds, and that they were awa' whenever they got a chance wi' Maister Fothergill West tae Branksome, but the general was too fu' o' his ain troubles tae ken aboot it, and it didna' seem tae me that it was pairt o' my duties either as coach-man or as gaird'ner tae mind the bairns. He should have lairned that if ye forbid a lassie and a laddie to dae anything it's just the surest way o' bringin' it aboot. The Lord foond that oot in the gairdin o' Paradise, and there's no muckle change between the folk in Eden and the folk in Wigtown.

There's ane thing that I havena' spoke aboot yet, but that should be set doon. The general didna' share his room wi' his wife, but slept a' alane in a chamber at the far end o' the hoose, as distant as possible frae every one else. This room was aye lockit when he wasna' in it, and naebody was ever allowed tae gang into it. He would mak' his ain bed, and red it up and dust it a' by himself, but he wouldna' so much as allow one o' us to set fut on the passage that led tae it. At nicht he would walk a' ower the hoose, and he had lamps hung in every room and cor-ner, so that no pairt should be dark. Many's the time frae my room in the garret I've heard his futsteps comin' and gangin', comin' and gangin', doun one passage and up anither, frae midnight till cockcraw. It was weary wark to lie listenin' tae his clatter and wonderin' whether he was clean daft, or whether maybe he'd learned pagan and idolatrous tricks oot in India, and that his conscience noo was like the worm which gnaweth and dieth not. I'd ha' speered frae him whether it wouldna' ease him to speak wi' the holy Donald McSnaw, but it might ha' been a mistake, and the general wasna' a man that you'd care tae mak' a mistake wi'.

Ane day I was workin' at the grass border when he comes up and he says, says he, "Did ye ever have occasion tae fire a pistol, Israel?"

"Godsakes!" says I, "I never had siccan a thing in my honds in my life."

"Then you'd best not begin noo," says he. "Every man tae his ain weepon," he says. "Now I warrant ye could dae something wi' a guid crab-tree cudgel!"

"Aye, could I," I answered, blithely, "as weel as ony lad on the border."

"This is a lonely hoose," says he, "and we might be molested by some rascals. It's weel tae be ready for whatever may come. Me and you and my son Mordaunt and Mr. Fothergill West, of Branksome, who would come if he was required, ought tae be able tae show a bauld face—what think ye?"

"'Deed, sir," I says, "feastin' is aye better than fechtin'—but if ye'll raise me a pund a month, I'll no shirk my share o' either."

"We won't quarrel ower that," says he, and agreed tae the extra twal' pund a year as easy as though it were as many bawbees. Far be it frae me tae think evil, but I couldna' help surmisin' at the time that money that was so lightly pairted wi' was maybe no very honestly cam' by.

"I'm no' a curious or a pryin' mun by nature, but I was sair puzzled in my aim mind tae tell why it was that the general walked aboot at nicht and what kept him frae his sleep. Well, a'e day I was cleanin' down the passages when my e'e fell on a great muckle heap o' curtains and auld cairpets and sic' like things that were piled away in a corner, no vera far frae the door o' the general's room. A' o' a sudden a thocht cam' intae my heid and I says tae mysel', "Israel, laddie," says I, "what's tae stop ye frae hidin' behind that this vera nicht and seein' the auld mun when he doesna' ken human e'e is on him?" The mair I thocht o't the mair seemple it appeared, and I made up my mind tae put the idea intae instant execution.

When the nicht cam' roond I tauld the womenfolk that I was bad wi' the jawache, and would gang airly tae my room. I kenned fine when ance I got there that there was na chance o' ony one disturbin' me, so I waited a wee while, and then when a' was quiet, I slippit aff my boots and ran doun the ither stair until I cam' tae the heap o' auld clothes, and there I lay doun wi' one e'e peepin' through a kink and a' the rest covered up wi' a great ragged cairpet. There I bided as quiet as a rotten until the general passed me on his road tae bed, and a' was still in the house.

My certie! I wouldna' gang through wi' it again for a' the siller at the Union Bank o' Dumfries! I canna think o't noo withoot feelin' cauld a' the way doun my back. It was just awfu' lyin' there in the deid silence, waitin' and waitin' wi' never a soond tae break the monotony, except the heavy tickin' o' an auld clock somewhere doun the passage. First I would look doun the corridor in the one way, and syne I'd look doun in t'ither, but it aye seemed to me as though there was something coming up frae the side that I wasna' lookin' at. I had a cauld sweat on my broo and my hairt was beatin' twice tae ilka tick o' the clock, and what feared me most of a' was that the dust frae the curtains and things was aye gettin' doun into my lungs and it was a' I could dae tae keep mysel' frae coughin'. Godsakes! I wonder my hair wasna' grey wi' a' that I went through! I wouldna' dae it again to be made Lord Provost o' Glasgie!

Well, it may have been twa o'clock in the mornin' or maybe a little mair, and I was just thinkin' that I wasna' tae see onything after a'—and I wasna' very sorry neither—when all o' a sudden a soond cam' tae my ears clear and distinct through the stillness o' the nicht. I've been asked afore noo tae describe that soond, but I've aye foond that it's no' vera easy tae gie a clear idea o't, though it was unlike any other soond that ever I hearkened tae. It was a shairp ringin' clang, like what could be caused by flippin' the rim o' a wine glass, but it was far higher and thinner than that and had in it tae a kind o' splash, like the tingle o' a rain-drop intae a waterbutt. In my fear I sat up amang my cairpets, like a puddock among gowan-leaves, and I listened wi' a' my ears. A' was still again noo, except for the dull tickin' o' the distant clock.

Suddenly the soond cam' again, as clear, as shrill, as shairp as ever, and this time the general heard it, for I heard him gie a kind o' groan, as a tired man might wha has been roosed oot o' his sleep. He got up frae his bed, and I could make oot a rustling noise, as though he were dressin' himsel', and presently his footfa' as he begun tae walk up and doun in his room. My sakes! it didna tak' lang for me tae drap doun amang the cairpets again and cover mysel' ower! There I lay tremblin' in every limb, and sayin' as mony prayers as I could mind, wi' my e'e still peepin' through the keek-hole, and fixed upon the door o' the general's room.

I heard the rattle o' the handle presently, and the door swung slowly open. There was a licht burnin' in the room beyond, an' I could just catch a glimpse o' what seemed tae me like a row o' swords stuck alang the side o' the wa', when the general stepped oot and shut the door behind him. He was dressed in a dressin' goon, wi' a red smokin'-cap on his heid, and a pair o' slippers wi' the heels cut off and the taes turned up. For a moment it cam' into my heid that maybe he was walkin' in his sleep, but as he cam' towards me I could see the glint o' the licht in his e'en, and his face was a' twistin', like a man that's in sair distress o' mind. On my conscience it gies me the shakes noo when I think o' his tall figure and his yelley face comin' sae solemn and silent doun the lang, lone passage. I haud my breath and lay close watchin' him, but just as he cam' tae where I was my vera hairt stood still in my breast, for "ting!"—lood and clear, within a yaird o' me cam the ringin', clangin' soond that I had a'ready hairkened tae. Where it cam' frae is mair than I can tell, or what was the cause o't. It might ha' been that the general made it, but I was sair puzzled tae tell hoo, for his honds were baith doun by his side as he passed me. It cam' frae his direction, certainly, but it appeared tae me tae come frae ower his heid; but it was siccan a thin, eerie, high-pitched, uncanny kind o' soond that it wasna' easy tae say just exactly where it did come frae. The general tak' nae heed o't, but walked on and was soon oot o' sicht, and I didna' lose a minute in creepin' oot frae my hidin' place and scamperin' awa' back tae my room, and if a' the bogies in the Red Sea were trapesin' up and doun the hale nicht through, I wud never put my heid oot again tae hae a glimpse o' them.

I didna' say a word tae anybody aboot what I'd seen, but I made up my mind that I wudna' stay muckle langer at Cloomber Ha'. Four pund a month is a good wage, but it isna' enough tae pay a man for the loss o' his peace o' mind, and maybe the loss o' his soul as weel, for when the deil is aboot ye canna' tell what sort o' a trap he may lay for ye, and though they say that Providence is stronger than him, it's maybe as weel no to risk it. It was clear tae me that the general and his hoose were baith under some curse, and it was fit that that curse should fa' on them that had earned it, and no' on a righteous Presbyterian, wha had ever trod the narrow path. My hairt was sair for young Miss Gabriel—for she was a bonnie and a winsome lassie—but for a' that, I felt that my duty was tae mysel' and that I should gang forth, even as Lot ganged oot o' the wicked cities o' the plain. That awfu' cling-clang was aye dingin' in my lugs, and I couldna' bear to be alane in the passages for fear o' hearin' it ance again. I only wanted a chance or an excuse tae gie the general notice, and tae gang back to some place where I could see Christian folk, and have the kirk within a stone-cast tae fa' back upon.

But it proved to be ordained that instead o' my saying the word, it should come frae the general himsel'. It was a'e day aboot the end of September, I was comin' oot o' the stable, after giein' its oats tae the horse, when I seed a great muckle loon come hoppin' on ane leg up the drive, mair like a big, ill-faured craw than a man. When I clapped my e'en on him I thocht that maybe this was ane of the rascals that the maister had been speakin' aboot, so withoot mair ado I fetched oot my bit stick with the intention o' tryin' it upon the limmer's heid. He seed me comin' towards him, and readin' my intention frae my look maybe, or frae the stick in my hand, he pu'ed oot a lang knife frae his pocket and swore wi' the most awfu' oaths that if I didna' stan' back he'd be the death o' me. Ma conscience, the words the chiel used was eneugh tae mak' the hair stand straight on your heid! I wonner he wasna' struck deid where he stood. We were still stanin' opposite each ither—he wi' his knife and me wi' the stick—when the general he cam' up the drive and foond us. Tae my surprise he began tae talk tae the stranger as if he'd kenned him a' his days.

"Put your knife in your pocket, corporal," says he. "Your fears have turned your brain."

"Blood an' wounds!" says the other. "He'd ha' turned my brain tae some purpose wi' that muckle stick o' his if I hadna' drawn my snickersnee. You shouldna' keep siccan an auld savage on your premises."

The maister he frooned and looked black at him as though he didna' relish advice comin' frae such a source. Then turnin' tae me, "You won't be wanted after to-day, Israel," he says; "you have been a guid servant and I ha' naething tae complain of wi' ye, but circumstances have arisen which will cause me tae change my arrangements." "Vera guid, sir," says I. "You can go this evening," says he, "and you shall have an extra month's pay tae mak' up t'ye for this short notice." Wi' that he went intae the hoose, followed by the man that he ca'ed the corporal, and frae that day tae this I have never clapped e'en either on the ane or the ither. My money was sent oot tae me in an envelope, and havin' said a few pairtin' words tae the cook and the wench wi' reference tae the wrath tae come and the treasure that is richer than rubies, I shook the dust o' Cloomber frae my feet for ever.

Maister Fothergill West says I maunna' express an opeenion as tae what cam' aboot afterwards, but maun confine mysel' tae what I saw mysel'. Nae doobt he has his reasons for this—and far be it frae me tae hint that they are no guid anes—but I maun say this, that what happened didna' surprise me. It was just as I expeckit, and so I said to Maister Donald McSnaw, I've tauld ye a' aboot it noo, and I havena' a word tae add or tae withdraw. I'm muckle obleeged tae Maister Mathew Clairk for puttin' it a' doun in writin' for me, and if there's ony would wish tae speer onything mair o' me I'm well kenned and respeckit in Ecclefechan, and Maister McNeil, the factor o' Wigtown, can aye tell where I am tae be foond.

CHAPTER IX

NARRTIVE OF JOHN EASTERLING, F.R.C.P. EDIN

HAVING given the statement of Israel Stakes *in extenso*, I shall now append a short memorandum from Dr. Easterling, now practising at Stranraer. It is true that the doctor was only once within the walls of Cloomber during its tenancy by General Heatherstone, but there were some circumstances connected with this visit which made it valuable, especially when considered as a supplement to the experiences which I have just submitted to the reader. The doctor has found time amid the calls of a busy country practise to jot down his recollections, and I feel that I cannot do better than subjoin them exactly as they stand.

I HAVE very much pleasure in furnishing Mr. Fothergill West with an account of my solitary visit to Cloomber Hall, not only on account of the esteem which I have formed for that gentleman ever since his residence at Branksome, but also because it is my conviction that the facts in the case of General Heatherstone are of such a singular nature that it is of the highest importance that they should be placed before the public in a trustworthy manner.

It was about the beginning of September of the year before last, that I received a note from Mrs. Heatherstone, of Cloomber Hall, desiring me to make a professional call upon her husband, whose health, she said, had been for some time in a very unsatisfactory state. I had heard something of the Heatherstones and of the strange seclusion in which they lived, so that I was very much pleased at this opportunity of making their closer acquaintance, and lost no time in complying with her request. I had known the Hall in the old days of Mr. McVittie, the original proprietor, and I was astonished on arriving at the avenue gate to observe the changes which had taken place. The gate itself, which used to yawn so hospitably upon the road, was now barred and locked, and a high wooden fence with nails upon the top encircled the whole grounds. The drive itself was leaf-strewn and uncared for, and the whole place had a depressing air of neglect and decay.

I had to knock twice before a servant-maid opened the door and showed me through a dingy hall into a small room, where sat an elderly, care-worn lady, who introduced herself as Mrs. Heatherstone. With her pale face, her grey hair, her sad, color-less eyes and her faded silk dress, she was in perfect keeping with her melancholy surroundings.

"You find us in much trouble, doctor," she said in a quiet, refined voice. "My poor husband has had a great deal to worry him, and his nervous system for a long time has been in a very weak state. We came to this part of the country in the hope that the bracing air and the quiet would have a good effect upon him. Instead of improving, however, he has seemed to grow weaker, and this morning he is in a high fever and a little in-clined to be delirious. The children and I were so frightened that we sent for you at once. If you will follow me I will take you to the general's bedroom."

She led the way down a series of corridors to the chamber of the sick man, which was situated in the extreme wing of the building. It was a carpetless, bleak-looking room, scantily fur-nished with a small truckle-bed, a campaigning chair, and a plain deal table, on which were scattered numerous papers and books. In the centre of this table there stood a large object of irregular outline which was covered over with a sheet of linen. All round the walls and in the corners were arranged a very choice and varied collection of arms, principally swords, some of which were of the straight pattern in common use in the British army, while among the others were scimitars, tulwars, cuchur-ries, and a score of other specimens of Oriental workmanship. Many of these were richly mounted with inlaid sheaths and hilts sparkling with precious stones, so that there was a piquant contrast between the simplicity of the apartment and the wealth which glittered on the walls. I had little time, however, to observe the general's collection, since the general himself lay upon his couch and was evidently in sore need of my services.

He was lying with his head turned half away from us, breathing heavily, and apparently unconscious of our presence. His bright, staring eyes and the deep, hectic flush upon his cheek showed that his fever was at its height. I advanced to the bedside, and, stooping over him, I placed my fingers upon his pulse, when immediately he sprang up into the sitting position and struck at me frenziedly with his clenched hands. I have never seen such intensity of fear and horror stamped upon a human face as appeared upon that which was now glaring up at me.

"Bloodhound!" he yelled; "let me go—let me go, I say! Keep your hands off me. Is it not enough that my life has been ruined? When is it all to end? How long am I to endure it?"

"Hush, dear, hush!" said his wife in a soothing voice, passing her cool hand over his heated forehead. "This is Doctor Easterling, from Stranraer. He has not come to harm you, but to do you good."

The general dropped wearily back upon his pillow, and I could see by the changed expression of his face that the delirium had left him and that he understood what had been said. I slipped my clinical thermometer into his armpit and counted his pulse rate. It amounted to 120 per minute, and his temperature proved to be 104 degrees. Clearly it was a case of remittent fever, such as occurs in men who have spent a great part of their lives in the tropics. "There is no danger," I remarked. "With a little quinine and arsenic we shall very soon overcome the attack and restore his health."

"No danger, eh!" he said. "There never is any danger for me. I am as hard to kill as the Wandering Jew. I am quite clear in the head now, Mary; so you may leave me with the doctor."

Mrs. Heatherstone left the room—rather unwillingly, as I thought—and I sat down by the bedside to listen to anything which my patient might have to communicate.

"I want you to examine my liver," he said, when the door was closed. "I used to have an abscess there, and Brodie, the staff-surgeon, said that it was ten to one that it would carry me off. I have not felt much of it since I left the East. This is where it used to be, just under the angle of the ribs."

"I can find the place," said I, after making a careful examination; "but I am happy to tell you that the abscess has either been entirely absorbed or has turned calcareous, as these solitary abscesses will. There is no fear of its doing you any harm now."

He seemed to be by no means overjoyed at the intelligence.

"Things always happen so with me," he said, moodily. "Now, if another fellow was feverish and delirious he would surely be in some danger; and yet you will tell me that I am in none. Look at this, now." He bared his chest and showed me a puckered wound over the region of the heart. "That's where the Jezail bullet of a hillman went in. You would think that was in the right spot to settle a man; and yet what does it do but glance upon a rib, and go clean round and out at the back, without so much as penetrating what you medicos call the pleura. Did ever you hear of such a thing?"

"You were certainly born under a lucky star," I observed with a smile.

"That's a matter of opinion," he answered, shaking his head. "Death has no terrors for me, if it will but come in some familiar form; but I confess that the anticipation of some strange, some preternatural form of death, is very terrible and unnerving."

"You mean," said I, rather puzzled at his remark, "that you would prefer a natural death to a death by violence."

"No, I don't mean that exactly," he answered. "I am too familiar with cold steel and lead to be afraid of either. Do you know anything about odyllic force, doctor?"

"No, I do not," I replied, glancing sharply at him to see if there were any signs of his delirium returning.

His expression was intelligent, however, and the feverish flush had faded from his cheeks.

"Ah, you western scientific men are very much behind the day in some things," he remarked. "In all that is material and conducive to the comfort of the body you are pre-eminent, but in what concerns the subtle forces of nature and the latent powers of the human spirit, your best men are centuries behind the humblest coolies of India. Countless generations of beef-eating, comfort-loving ancestors have given our animal instincts the command over our spiritual ones. The body, which should have been a mere tool for the use of the soul, has now become a degrading prison in which it is confined. The Oriental soul and body is not so welded together as ours is, and there is far less wrench when they part in death."

"They do not appear to derive much benefit from this peculiarity in their organization," I remarked, incredulously.

"Merely the benefit of superior knowledge," the general answered. "If you were to go to India, probably the very first thing you would see in the way of amusement would be a native doing what is called the mango trick. Of course you have heard or read of it. The fellow plants a mango seed and makes passes over it until it sprouts and bears leaves and fruit—all in the space of half an hour. It is not really a trick—it is a power. These men know more than your Tyndalls or Huxleys do about Nature's processes, and they can accelerate or retard her workings by subtle means, of which we have no conception. These low-caste *conjurros*—as they are called—are mere vulgar dabblers, but the men who have trod the higher path, the brethren of the Ragi-zog, are far more our superiors in knowledge than we are of the Hottentots or Patagonians."

"You speak as if you were well acquainted with them," I remarked.

"To my cost, I do," he answered. "I have been brought in contact with them in a way in which I trust no other poor devil ever will be. But, really, as regards odyllic force you ought to know something of it, for it has a great future before it in your profession. You should read Reichenbach's "Researches on Magnetism and Vital Force,' and Gregory's 'Letters on Animal Magnetism.' These supplemented by the twenty-seven Aphorisms of Mesmer, and the works of Dr. Justinus Kerner, of Weinsberg, would enlarge your ideas."

I did not particularly relish having a course of reading prescribed for me on a subject connected with my own profession, so I made no comment, but rose to take my departure. Before doing so I felt his pulse once more, and found that the fever had entirely left him, in the sudden, unaccountable fashion which is peculiar to these malarious types of disease. I turned my face towards him to congratulate him upon his improvement, and stretched out my hand at the same time to pick my gloves from the table, with the result that I raised not only my own property, but also the linen cloth which was arranged over some object in the centre. I might not have noticed what I had done had I not seen an angry look upon the invalid's face and heard him utter an impatient exclamation. I at once turned, and replaced the cloth so promptly that I should have been unable to say what was underneath it, beyond having a general impression that it looked like a bride-cake.

"All right, doctor," the general said good-humoredly, perceiving how entirely accidental the incident was. "There is no reason why you should not see it," and stretching out his hand, he pulled away the linen covering for the second time. I then perceived that what I had taken for a bride-cake was really an admirably executed model of a lofty range of mountains, whose snow-clad peaks were not unlike the familiar sugar pinnacles and minarets.

"These are the Himalayas, or at least the Surinam branch of them," he remarked, "showing the principal passes between India and Afghanistan. It is an excellent model. This ground has a special interest for me, because it is the scene of my first campaign. There is the pass opposite Kalabagh and the Thul valley, where I was engaged during the summer of 1841, in protecting the convoys and keeping the Afridis in order. It wasn't a sinecure I promise you."

"And this," said I, indicating a blood-red spot which had been marked on one side of the pass which he had pointed out—"this is the scene of some fight in which you were engaged."

"Yes, we had a skirmish there," he answered, leaning forward and looking at the red mark. "We were attacked by—" At this moment he fell back upon his pillow as if he had been shot, while the same look of horror came over his face which I had observed when I first entered the room. At the same instant there came, apparently from the air immediately above his bed, a sharp, ringing, tinkling sound, which I can only compare to the noise made by a bicycle alarm, though it differed from this in having a distinctly throbbing character. I have never, before or since, heard any sound which could be confounded with it. I stared round in astonishment, wondering where it could have come from, but without perceiving anything to which it could be ascribed.

"It's all right, doctor," the general said, with a forced smile. "It's only my private gong. Perhaps you had better step downstairs and write my prescription in the dining-room.

He was evidently anxious to get rid of me; so I was forced to take my departure, though I would gladly have stayed a little longer, in the hope of learning something as to the origin of the mysterious sound. I drove away from the house with the full determination of calling again upon my interesting patient, and endeavoring to elicit some further particulars as to his past life and his present circumstances. I was destined, however, to be disappointed; for I received that very evening a note from the general himself, inclosing a handsome fee for my single visit, and informing me that my treatment had done him so much good that he considered himself to be convalescent, and would not trouble me to see him again. This was the last and the only communication which I ever received from the tenant of Cloomber.

I have been frequently asked by neighbors and others who were interested in the matter, whether he gave me the impression of insanity. To this I must unhesitatingly answer in the negative. On the contrary his remarks gave me the idea of a man who had both read and thought deeply. I observed, however, during our single interview, that his reflexes were feeble, his arcus senilis well-marked, and his arteries atheromatous—all signs that his constitution was in an unsatisfactory condition, and that a sudden crisis might be apprehended.

CHAPTER X

OF THE LETTER WHICH CAME FROM THE HALL

Having thrown this side-light upon my narrative, I can now resume the statement of my own personal experiences. These I had brought down, as the reader will doubtless remember, to the date of the arrival of the savage-looking wanderer who called himself Corporal Rufus Smith. This incident occurred about the close of the month of September, and I find upon a comparison of dates that Dr. Easterling's visit to Cloomber preceded it by three weeks or more. During all this time I was in sore distress of mind, for I had never seen anything either of Gabriel or of her brother since the interview in which the general had discovered the communication which was kept up between us. I had no doubt that some sort of restraint had been placed upon them; and the thought that we had brought trouble on their heads was a bitter one both to my sister and myself.

Our anxiety, however, was considerably mitigated by the receipt, a couple of days after my last talk with the general, of a note from Mordaunt Heatherstone. This was brought us by a little ragged urchin, the son of one of the fishermen, who informed us that it had been handed to him at the avenue gate by an old woman—who, I expect, must have been the Cloomber cook.

"My dearest friends," it ran, "Gabriel and I have grieved to think how concerned you must be at having neither heard from or seen us. The fact is that we are compelled to remain in the house. And this compulsion is not physical but moral. Our poor father, who gets more and more nervous every day, has entreated us to promise him that we will not go out until after the

5th of October, and to allay his fears we have given him the desired pledge. On the other hand, he has promised us that after the 5th—that is, in less than a week—we shall be as free as air to come or go as we please; so we have something to look forward to. Gabriel says that she has explained to you that the governor is always a changed man after this particular date, on which his fears reach a crisis. He apparently has more reason than usual this year to anticipate that trouble is brewing for this unfortunate family, for I have never known him to take so many elaborate precautions or appear so thoroughly unnerved. Who would ever think, to see his bent form and his shaking hands, that he is the same man who used some few short years ago to shoot tigers on foot among the jungles of the Terai, and would laugh at the more timid sportsmen who sought the protection of their elephant's howdah? You know that he has the Victoria Cross, which he won in the streets of Delhi, and yet here he is shivering with terror and starting at every noise, in the most peaceful corner of the world. Oh, the pity of it, West! Remember what I have already told you—that it is no fanciful or imaginary peril, but one which we have every reason to suppose to be most real. It is, however, of such a nature that it can neither be averted nor can it profitably be expressed in words. If all goes well, you will see us at Branksome on the 6th. With our fondest love to both of you, I am ever, my dear friends, your attached.

MORDAUNT."

This letter was a great relief to us as letting us know that the brother and sister were under no physical restraint; but our powerlessness and inability even to comprehend what the danger was which threatened those whom we had come to love better than ourselves was little short of maddening. Fifty times a day we asked ourselves and asked each other from what possible quarter this peril was to be expected; but the more we thought of it the more hopeless did any solution appear. In vain we combined our experiences and pieced together every word which had fallen from the lips of any inmate of Cloomber which might be supposed to bear directly or indirectly upon the subject. At last, weary with fruitless speculation, we were fain to try

and drive the matter from our thoughts, consoling ourselves
with the reflection that in a few more days all restrictions would
be removed, and we should be able to learn from our friends'
own lips. Those few intervening days, however, would, we
feared, be dreary, long ones. And so they would, had it not been
for a new and most unexpected incident, which diverted our
minds from our own troubles and gave them something fresh
with which to occupy themselves.

CHAPTER XI

OF THE CASTING AWAY OF THE BARK "BELINDA"

OCTOBER had broken auspiciously with a bright sun and a cloudless sky. There had in the morning been a slight breeze, and a few little white wreaths of vapor drifted here and there like the scattered feathers of some gigantic bird; but as the day wore on, such wind as there was fell completely away, and the air became close and stagnant. The sun blazed down with a degree of heat which was remarkable so late in the season, and a shimmering haze lay upon the upland moors and concealed the Irish mountains on the other side of the Channel. The sea itself rose and fell in a long, heavy, oily roll, sweeping slowly landward, and breaking sullenly with a dull, monotonous booming upon the rock-girt shore. To the inexperienced all seemed calm and peaceful, but to those who are accustomed to read Nature's warnings there was a dark menace in air and sky and sea.

My sister and I walked out in the afternoon, sauntering slowly along the margin of the great, sandy spit which shoots out into the Irish Sea, flanking upon one side the magnificent Bay of Luce, and on the other the more obscure inlet of Kirkmaiden, on the shores of which the Branksome property is situated. It was too sultry to go far; so we soon seated ourselves upon one of the sandy hillocks, overgrown with faded grass-tufts, which extend along the coast-line, and which form Nature's dykes against the encroachments of the ocean. Our rest was soon interrupted by the scrunching of heavy boots upon the shingle; and Jamieson, the old man-o'-war's man whom I have already had occasion to mention, made his appearance, with the flat, circular net upon his back which he used for shrimp-catching. He came towards us upon seeing us, and said in his rough, kindly way that he hoped we would not take it amiss if he sent us up a dish of shrimps for our tea at Branksome. "I aye make a good catch before a storm," he remarked.

"You think there is going to be a storm, then?" I asked.

"Why, even a marine could see that," he answered, sticking a great wedge of tobacco into his cheek. "The moors over near Cloomber are just white wi' gulls and kittiwakes. What d'ye think they come ashore for except to escape having all the feathers blown out o' them? I mind a day like this when I was wi' Charlie Napier off Cronstadt. It well nigh blew us under the guns of the forts, for all our engines and propellers."

"Have you ever known a wreck in these parts?" I asked.

"Lord love ye, sir, it's a famous place for wrecks. Why, in that very bay down there two o' King Philip's first-rates foundered wi' all hands in the days o' the Spanish war. If that sheet o' water and the Bay o' Luce round the corner could tell their ain tale they'd have a gey lot to speak of. When the Jedgment Day comes round that water will be just bubbling wi' the number o' folks that will be coming up frae the bottom."

"I trust that there will be no wrecks while we are here," said Esther, earnestly.

The old man shook his grizzled head and looked distrustfully at the hazy horizon. "If it blows from the west," he said, "some o' these sailing ships may find it no joke to be caught without sea-room in the North Channel. There's that bark out there—I daresay her maister would be glad enough to find himself safe in the Clyde."

"She seems to be absolutely motionless," I remarked, looking at the vessel in question, whose black hull and gleaming sails rose and fell slowly with the throbbing of the giant pulse beneath her. "Perhaps, Jamieson, we are wrong, and there will be no storm after all."

The old sailor chuckled to himself with an air of superior knowledge, and shuffled away with his shrimp-net, while my sister and I walked slowly homeward through the hot and stagnant air. I went up to my father's study to see if the old gentleman had any instructions as to the estate, for he had become engrossed in a new work upon Oriental literature, and the practical management of the property had in consequence devolved entirely upon me.

I found him seated at his square library table, which was so heaped with books and papers that nothing of him was visible from the door except a tuft of white hair. "My dear son," he said to me as I entered, "it is a great grief to me that you are not more conversant with Sanscrit. When I was your age, I could converse not only in that noble language, but also in the Tamulic, Lohitic, Gangelic, Taic, and Malaic dialects, which are all offshoots from the Turanian branch."

"I regret extremely, sir," I answered, "that I have not inherited your wonderful talents as a polyglot."

"I have set myself a task," he explained, "which, if it could only be continued from generation to generation in our own family until it was completed, would make the name of West immortal. This is nothing less than to publish an English translation of the Buddhist Djarmas, with a preface giving an idea of the position of Brahminism before the coming of Sakyamuni. With diligence it is possible that I might be able myself to complete part of the preface before I die."

"And pray, sir," I asked, "how long would the whole work be when it was finished?"

"The abridged edition in the Imperial Library of Pekin," said my father, rubbing his hands together, "consists of 325 volumes of an average weight of five pounds. Then the preface, which must embrace some account of the Rig-veda, the Sáma-veda, the Yagur-veda and the Atharva-veda, with the Brahmanas, could hardly be completed in less than ten volumes. Now if we apportion one volume to each year there is every prospect of the family coming to an end of its task about the date 2250, the twelfth generation completing the work, while the thirteenth might occupy itself upon the index."

"And how are our descendants to live, sir." I asked with a smile, "during the progress of this great undertaking?"

"That's the worst of you, Jack," my father cried, petulantly. "There is nothing practical about you. Instead of confining your attention to the working out of my noble scheme, you begin raising all sorts of absurd objections. It is a mere matter of detail how our descendants live, so long as they stick to the Djarmas. Now I want you to go up to the bothy of Fergus McDonald and see about the thatch, and Willie Fullerton has written to say that his milk-cow is bad. You might look in upon your way and ask after it."

I started off upon my errands, but before doing so I took a look at the barometer upon the wall. The mercury had sunk to the phenomenal point of twenty-eight inches. Clearly the old sailor had not been wrong in his interpretation of Nature's signs. As I returned over the moors in the evening the wind was blowing in short, angry puffs, and the western horizon was heaped with sombre clouds which stretched their long, ragged tentacles right up to the zenith. Against their dark background one or two livid, sulphur-colored splotches showed up malignant and menacing, while the surface of the sea had changed from the appearance of burnished quicksilver to that of ground glass. A low, moaning sound rose up from the ocean as if it knew that trouble was in store for it. Far out in the Channel I saw a single panting, eager steam-vessel making its way to Belfast Lough, and the large bark which I had observed in the morning still beating about in the offing, endeavoring to pass to the northward. At nine o'clock a sharp breeze was blowing; at ten it had freshened into a gale; and before midnight the most furious storm was raging which I can remember upon that weather-beaten coast.

I sat for some time in our small, oak-panelled sitting-room listening to the screeching and howling of the blast and to the rattle of the gravel and pebbles as they pattered against the window. Nature's grim orchestra was playing its world-old piece with a compass which ranged from the deep diapason of the thundering surge to the thin shriek of the scattered shingle and the keen piping of frightened sea birds. Once for an instant I opened the lattice window, but a gust of wind and rain came blustering through, bearing with it a great sheet of sea-weed, which flapped down upon the table. It was all I could do to close it again in the face of the blast. My sister and my father had retired to their rooms, but my thoughts were too active for sleep, so I continued to sit and to smoke by the smoldering fire.

What was going on in the Hall now, I wondered? What did Gabriel think of the storm, and how did it affect the old man who wandered about in the night? Did he welcome these dread forces of nature as being of the same order of things as his own tumultuous thoughts? It was only four days now from the date which I had been assured was to mark a crisis in his fortunes. Would he regard this sudden tempest as being in any way connected with the mysterious fate which threatened him? Over all these things and many more I pondered as I sat by the glowing embers until they died gradually out, and the chill night air warned me that it was time to retire.

I may have slept a couple of hours when I was awoke by some one tugging furiously at my shoulder. Sitting up in bed, I saw by the dim light that my father was standing half clad by my bedside, and that it was his grasp which I felt on my night-shirt.

"Get up, Jack, get up!" he was crying excitedly. "There's a great ship ashore in the bay, and the poor folk will all be drowned. Come down, my boy, and let us see what we can do." The good old man seemed to be nearly beside himself with excitement and impatience.

I sprang from my bed, and was huddling on a few clothes, when a dull, booming sound made itself heard above the howling of the wind and the thunder of the breakers.

"There it is again!" cried my father. "It is their signal gun, poor creatures! Jamieson and the fishermen are below. Put your oilskin coat on and the Glengarry hat. Come, come, every second may mean a human life!" We hurried down together and made our way to the beach, accompanied by a dozen or so of the inhabitants of Branksome.

The gale had increased rather than moderated, and the wind screamed all round us with an infernal clamor. So great was its force that we had to put our shoulders against it, and bore our way through it, while the sand and gravel tingled up against our faces. There was just light enough to make out the scudding clouds and the white gleam of the breakers, but beyond that all was absolute darkness. We stood ankle deep in the shingle and seaweed, shading our eyes with our hands and peering out into the inky obscurity. It seemed to me as I listened that I could hear human voices loud in entreaty and terror, but amid the wild turmoil of nature it was difficult to distinguish one sound from another. Suddenly, however, a light glimmered in the heart of the tempest, and next instant the beach and sky and wide tossing bay were brilliantly illuminated by the wide glare of a signal light.

She lay on her beam ends right in the centre of the terrible Hansel reef, hurled over to such an angle that I could see all the planking of her deck. I recognized her at once as being the same three-masted bark which I had observed in the Channel in the morning, and the Union Jack which was nailed upside down to the jagged stump of her mizzen proclaimed her nationality. Every spar and rope and writhing piece of cordage showed up hard and clear under the livid light which sputtered and flickered from the highest portion of the forecastle. Beyond the doomed ship out of the great darkness came the long, rolling lines of black waves, never ending, never tiring, with a petulant tuft of foam here and there upon their crests. Each as it reached the broad circle of unnatural light appeared to gather strength and volume and to hurry on more impetuously until with a roar and a jarring crash it sprang upon its victim. Clinging to the weather shrouds we could distinctly see ten or a dozen frightened seamen, who, when the light revealed our presence, turned their white faces towards us and waved their hands imploringly. The poor wretches had evidently taken fresh hope from our presence, though it was clear that their own boats had either been washed away or so damaged as to render them useless.

The sailors who clung to the rigging were not, however, the only unfortunates aboard. On the breaking poop there stood three men who appeared to be both of a different race and nature from the cowering wretches who implored our assistance. Leaning upon the shattered taffrail they seemed to be conversing together as quietly and unconcernedly as though they were unconscious of the deadly peril which surrounded them. As the signal light flickered over them we could see from the shore that these immutable strangers wore red fezes, and that their faces were all of a swarthy, large-featured type, which proclaimed an eastern origin. There was little time, however, for us to take note of such details. The ship was breaking rapidly, and some effort must be made to save the poor, sodden group of humanity who implored our assistance. The nearest lifeboat was in the Bay of Luce, ten long miles away, but here was our own broad, roomy craft upon the shingle, and plenty of brave fisher lads to form a crew. Six of us sprang to the oars, the others pushed us off, and we fought our way through the swirling, raging waters, staggering and recoiling before the great, sweeping billows, but still steadily decreasing the distance between the bark and ourselves.

It seemed, however, that our efforts were fated to be in vain. As we mounted upon a surge I saw a giant wave, topping all the others, and coming after them like a driver following a flock, sweep down upon the vessel, curling its great, green arch over the breaking deck. With a rending, riving sound the ship split in two, where the terrible serrated back of the Hansel reef was sawing into her keel. The after-part with the broken mizzen and the three Orientals sank backwards into deep water and vanished, while the fore-half oscillated helplessly about, retaining its precarious balance upon the rocks. A wail of fear went up from the wreck and was echoed from the beach, but by the blessing of Providence she kept afloat until we made our way under her bowsprit and rescued every man of the crew. We had not got half way upon our return, however, when another great wave swept the shattered forecastle off the reef, and extinguishing the signal light, hid the wild *dénouement* from our view.

Our friends upon the shore were loud in congratulation and praise, nor were they backward in welcoming and comforting the castaways. They were thirteen in all, as cold and cowed a set of mortals as ever slipped through Death's fingers, save indeed their captain, who was a hardy, robust man, and who made light of the affair. Some were taken off to this cottage and some to that, but the greater part came back to Branksome with us, where we gave them such dry clothes as we could lay our hands on, and served them with beef and beer by the kitchen fire. The captain, whose name was Meadows, compressed his bulky form into a suit of my own, and came down to the parlor, where he mixed himself some grog and gave my father and myself an account of the disaster.

"If it hadn't been for you, sir, and your brave fellows," he said, smiling across at me, "we should be ten fathom deep by this time. As to the 'Belinda,' she was a leaky old tub and well insured, so neither the owners nor I are likely to break our hearts over her."

"I am afraid," said my father, sadly, "that we shall never see your three passengers again. I have left men upon the beach in case they should be washed up, but I fear it is hopeless. I saw them go down when the vessel split, and no man could have lived for a moment among that terrible surge."

"Who were they?" I asked. "I could not have believed that it was possible for men to appear so unconcerned in the face of such imminent peril."

"As to who they are or were," the captain answered, puffing thoughtfully at his pipe, "that is by no means easy to say. Our last port was Kurrachee, in the north of India, and there we took them aboard as passengers for Glasgow, Ram Singh was the name of the younger, and it is only with him that I have come in contact, but they all appeared to be quiet, inoffensive gentlemen. I never inquired their business, but I should judge that they were Parsee merchants from Hyderabad, whose trade took them to Europe. I could never see why the crew should fear them, and the mate, too; he should have had more sense."

"Fear them!" I ejaculated in surprise.

"Yes, they had some preposterous idea that they were dangerous shipmates. I have no doubt if you were to go down into the kitchen now, you would find that they are all agreed that our passengers were the cause of the disaster."

As the captain was speaking, the parlor door opened, and the mate of the bark, a tall, red-bearded sailor, stepped in. He had obtained a complete rig-out from some kind-hearted fisherman, and looked in his comfortable jersey and well-greased sea-boots a very favorable specimen of a shipwrecked mariner. With a few words of grateful acknowledgment of our hospitality he drew a chair up to the fire and warmed his great, brown hands before the blaze.

"What d'ye think now, Captain Meadows," he asked presently, glancing up at his superior officer. "Didn't I warn you what would be the upshot of having those niggers on board the 'Belinda?'"

The captain leaned back in his chair and laughed heartily. "Didn't I tell you?" he cried, appealing to us. "Didn't I tell you?"

"It might have been no laughing matter for us," the other remarked, petulantly. "I have lost a good sea-kit and nearly lost my life into the bargain."

"Do I understand you to say," said I, "that you attribute your misfortunes to your ill-fated passengers?"

The mate opened his eyes at the adjective. "Why ill-fated, sir?" he asked.

"Because they are most certainly drowned," I answered.

He sniffed incredulously and went on warming his hands. "Men of that kind are never drowned," he said, after a pause. "Their father, the devil, looks after them. Did you see them standing on the poop and rolling cigarettes at the time when the mizzen was carried away and the quarter-boats stove? That was enough for me. I'm not surprised at you landsmen not being able to take it in, but the captain, here, who's been sailing since he was the height of the binnacle, ought to know by this time that a cat and a priest are the worst cargo you can carry. If a Christian priest is bad, I guess an idolatrous pagan one is fifty times worse. I stand by the old religion, and be d—d to it!"

My father and I could not help laughing at the rough sailor's very unorthodox way of proclaiming his orthodoxy. The mate, however, was evidently in deadly earnest, and proceeded to state his case, marking off the different points upon the rough, red fingers of his left hand.

"It was at Kurrachee, directly after they come, that I warned ye," he said, reproachfully, to the captain. "There was three Buddhist Lascars in my watch, and what did they do when them chaps come aboard? Why, they down on their stomachs and rubbed their noses on the deck—that's what they did. They wouldn't ha' done as much for an admiral of the R'yal Navy. They know who's who—these niggers do; and I smelled mischief the moment I saw them on their faces. I asked them afterwards in your presence, captain, why they had done it, and they answered that the passengers were holy men. You heard 'em yourself."

"Well, there's no harm in that, Hawkins," said Captain Meadows.

"I don't know that, the mate said, doubtfully. "The holiest Christian is the one that's nearest God, but the holiest nigger is, in my opinion, the one that's nearest the devil. Then you saw yourself, Captain Meadows, how they went on during the voyage, reading books that was writ on wood instead o' paper, and sitting up right through the night to jabber together on the quarter-deck. What did they want to have a chart of their own for and to mark the course of the vessel every day?

"They didn't," said the captain.

"Indeed they did, and if I did not tell you sooner it was because you were always ready to laugh at what I said about them. They had instruments o' their own—when they used them I can't say—but every day at noon they worked out the latitude and longitude, and marked out the vessel's position on a chart that was pinned on their cabin table. I saw them at it, and so did the steward from his pantry."

"Well, I don't see what you prove from that," the captain remarked, "though I confess it is a strange thing."

"I'll tell you another strange thing," said the mate, impressively. "Do you know the name of this bay in which we are cast away?"

"I have learned from our kind friends here that we are upon the Wigtownshire coast," the captain answered, "but I have not heard the name of the bay."

The mate leaned forward with a grave face. "It is the Bay of Kirkmaiden," he said.

If he expected to astonish Captain Meadows he certainly succeeded, for that gentleman was fairly bereft of speech for a minute or more. "That is really marvellous," he said, after a time, turning to us. "These passengers of ours cross-questioned us early in the voyage as to the existence of a bay of that name. Hawkins here and I denied all knowledge of one, for on the chart it is included in the Bay of Luce. That we should eventually be blown into it and destroyed is an extraordinary coincidence."

"Too extraordinary to be a coincidence," growled the mate. "I saw them during the calm yesterday morning, pointing to the land over our starboard quarter. They knew well enough that that was the port they were making for."

"What do you make of it all, then, Hawkins?" asked the captain with a troubled face; "what is your own theory on the matter?"

"Why, in my opinion," the mate answered, "them three swabs have no more difficulty in raising a gale o' wind than I should have in swallowing this here grog. They had reasons of their own for coming to this God-forsaken—saving your presence, sirs— this God-forsaken bay, and they took a short cut to it by arranging to be blown ashore there. That's my idea o' the matter, though what three Buddhist priests could find to do in the Bay of Kirkmaiden is clean past my comprehension."

My father raised his eyebrows to indicate the doubt which his hospitality forbade him from putting into words. "I think, gentlemen," he said, "that you are both sorely in need of rest after your perilous adventures. If you will follow me I shall lead you to your rooms." He conducted them with old-fashioned ceremony to the laird's best spare bedroom, and then returning to me in the parlor, proposed that we should go down together to the beach and learn whether anything fresh had occurred.

The first pale light of dawn was just appearing in the east when we made our way for the second time to the scene of the shipwreck. The gale had blown itself out, but the sea was still very high, and all inside the breakers was a seething, gleaming line of foam, as though the fierce old ocean was gnashing its white teeth at the victims who had escaped from its clutches. All along the beach the fishermen and crofters were hard at work hauling up spars and barrels as fast as they were tossed ashore. None of them had seen any bodies, however, and they explained to us that only such things as could float had any chance of coming ashore, for the undercurrent was so strong that whatever was beneath surface must infallibly be swept out to sea. As to the possibility of the unfortunate passengers having been able to reach the shore, these practical men would not hear of it for a moment, and showed us conclusively that if they had not been drowned they must have been dashed to pieces upon the rocks.

"We did all that could be done," my father said, as we returned home. "I am afraid that the poor mate has had his reason affected by the suddenness of the disaster. Did you hear what he said about Buddhist priests raising a gale?"

"Yes, I heard him," said I.

"It was very painful to listen to him," said my father. "I wonder if he would object to my putting a small mustard plaster under each of his ears. It would relieve any congestion of the brain. Or perhaps it would be best to wake him up and give him two antibilious pills. What do you think, Jack?"

"I think," said I with a yawn, "that you had best let him sleep, and go to sleep yourself. You can physic him in the morning if he needs it." So saying I stumbled off to my bedroom, and throwing myself upon the couch, was soon in a dreamless slumber.

CHAPTER XII

OF THE THREE FOREIGN MEN UPON THE COAST

IT must have been eleven or twelve o'clock before I work up, and it seemed to me, in the flood of golden light which streamed into my chamber, that the wild, tumultuous episodes of the night before must have formed part of some fantastic dream. It was hard to believe that the gentle breeze which whispered so softly among the ivy-leaves around my window was caused by the same element which had shaken the very house a few short hours before. It was as if Nature had repented of her momentary passion and was endeavoring to make amends to an injured world by its warmth and its sunshine. A chorus of birds in the garden below filled the whole air with their wonder and congratulations.

Down in the hall I found a number of the shipwrecked sailors, looking all the better for their night's repose, who set up a buzz of pleasure and gratitude upon seeing me. Arrangements had been made to drive them to Wigtown, whence they were to proceed to Glasgow by the evening train, and my father had given orders that each should be served with a packet of sandwiches and hard-boiled eggs to sustain him on the way. Captain Meadows thanked us warmly in the name of his employers for the manner in which we had treated them, and he called for three cheers from his crew, which were very heartily given. He and the mate walked down with us after we had broken our fast, to have a last look at the scene of his disaster.

The great bosom of the bay was still heaving convulsively, and its waves were breaking into sobs against the rocks, but there was none of that wild turmoil which we had seen in the early

morning. The long emerald ridges, with their smart little cock-
ades of foam, rolled slowly and majestically in, to break with a
regular rhythm—the panting of a tired monster. A cable length
from the shore, we could see the mainmast of the bark floating
upon the waves, disappearing at times in the trough of the sea,
and then shooting up towards heaven like a giant javelin, as the
rollers tossed it about. Other smaller pieces of wreckage dotted
the waters, while innumerable spars and packages were littered
over the sands. These were being drawn up and collected in a
place of safety by gangs of peasants. I noticed that a couple of
broad-winged gulls were hovering and skimming over the scene
of the shipwreck as though many strange things were visible to
them beneath the waves. At times we could hear their raucous
voices as they spoke to one another of what they saw.

"She was a leaky old craft," said the captain, looking sadly out
to sea; "but there's always a feeling of sorrow when we see the
last of a ship we have sailed in. Well, well, she would have been
broken up in any case, and sold for firewood."

"It looks a peaceful scene," I remarked. "Who would imagine
that three men lost their lives last night in those waters?"

"Poor fellows," said the captain, with feeling. "Should they be
cast up after our departure, I am sure, Mr. West, that you will
have them decently interred."

I was about to make some reply when the mate burst into a
loud guffaw, slapping his thigh and choking with merriment. "If
you want to bury them," he said, "you had best look sharp, or
they may clear out of the country. You remember what I said last
night. Just look at the top of that 'ere hillock, and tell me
whether I was in the right or not?"

There was a high sand dune some little distance along the
coast, and upon the summit of this the figure was standing
which had attracted the mate's attention. The captain threw up
his hands in astonishment as his eyes rested upon it. "By the
eternal," he shouted, "it's Ram Singh himself! Let us overhaul
him!" Taking to his heels in his excitement he raced along the
beach, followed by the mate and myself, as well as by one or two
of the fishermen who had observed the presence of the stranger.
The latter, perceiving our approach, came down from his post of

observation and walked quietly in our direction, with his head sunk upon his breast, like one who is absorbed in thought.

I could not help contrasting our hurried and tumultuous advance with the gravity and dignity of this lonely Oriental, nor was the matter mended when he raised a pair of steady, thoughtful dark eyes and inclined his head in a graceful, sweeping salutation. It seemed to me that we were like a pack of schoolboys in the presence of a master. The stranger's broad, unruffled brow, his clear, searching gaze, firm-set yet sensitive mouth, and clean-cut, resolute expression, all combined to form the most imposing and noble presence which I have ever known. I could not have imagined that such imperturbable calm and at the same time such a consciousness of latent strength could have been expressed by any human face. He was dressed in a brown velveteen coat, loose, dark trousers, with a shirt which was cut low in the collar, so as to show the muscular brow neck, and he still wore the red fez which I had noticed the night before. I observed with a feeling of surprise, as we approached him, that none of these garments showed the slightest indication of the rough treatment and wetting which they must have received during their wearer's submersion and struggle to the shore.

"So you are none the worse for your ducking," he said in a pleasant, musical voice, looking from the captain to the mate. "I hope that all your poor sailors have found pleasant quarters."

"We are all safe," the captain answered. "But we had given you up for lost—you and your two friends. Indeed I was just making arrangements for your burial with Mr. West here."

The stranger looked at me and smiled. "We won't give Mr. West that trouble for a little time yet," he remarked; "my friends and I came ashore all safe, and we have found shelter in a hut a mile or so down the coast. It is lonely down there, but we have everything which we can desire."

"We start for Glasgow this afternoon," said the captain; "I shall be very glad if you will come with us. If you have not been in England before you may find it awkward traveling alone."

"We are very much indebted to you for your thoughtfulness," Ram Singh answered; "but we will not take advantage of your kind offer. Since Nature has driven us here we intend to have a look about us before we leave."

"As you like," the captain said, shrugging his shoulders. "I don't think you are likely to find very much to interest you in this hole of a place."

"Very possibly not," Ram Singh answered with an amused smile. "You remember Milton's lines:

> 'The mind is its own place, and in itself
> Can make a hell of heaven, a heaven of hell.'

I daresay we can spend a few days here comfortably enough. Indeed, I think you must be wrong in considering this to be a barbarous locality. I am much mistaken if this young gentleman's father is not Mr. James Hunter West, whose name is known and honored by the pundits of India."

"My father is, indeed, a well-known Sanscrit scholar," I answered, in astonishment.

"The presence of such a man," observed the stranger, slowly, "changes a wilderness into a city. One great mind is surely a higher indication of civilization than are incalculable leagues of bricks, and mortar. Your father is hardly as profound as Sir William Jones, or as universal as the Baron Von Hammer-Purgstall, but he combines many of the virtues of each. You may tell him, however, from me that he is mistaken in the analogy which he has traced between the Samoyede and Tamulic word roots."

"If you have determined to honor our neighborhood by a short stay," said I, "you will offend my father very much if you do not put up with him. He represents the laird here, and it is the laird's privilege, according to our Scottish custom, to entertain all strangers of repute who visit his parish." My sense of hospitality prompted me to deliver this invitation, though I could feel the mate twitching at my sleeve as if to warn me that the offer was, for some reason, an objectionable one. His fears were, however, unnecessary, for the stranger signified by a shake of the head that it was impossible for him to accept it.

"My friends and I are very much obliged to you," he said, "but we have our own reasons for remaining where we are. The hut which we occupy is deserted and partly ruined, but we Easterns have trained ourselves to do without most of those things which are looked upon as necessaries in Europe, believing firmly in that wise axiom that a man is rich, not in proportion to what he has, but in proportion to what he can dispense with. A good fisherman supplies us with bread and with herbs, we have clean, dry straw for our couches, what could man wish for more?"

"But you must feel the cold at night, coming straight from the tropics," remarked the captain.

"Perhaps our bodies are cold sometimes. We have not noticed it. We have all three spent many years in the Upper Himalayas, on the border of the region of eternal snow, so we are not very sensitive to inconveniences of the sort."

"At least," said I, "you must allow me to send you over some fish and some meat from our larder."

"We are not Christians," he answered, "but Buddhists of the higher school. We do not recognize that man has a moral right to slay an ox or a fish for the gross use of his human body. He has not put life into them, and has assuredly no mandate from the Almighty to take life from them save under the most pressing needs. We could not, therefore, use your gift if you were to send it."

"But, sir," I remonstrated, "if in this changeable and inhospitable climate you refuse all nourishing food, your vitality will fail you—you will die."

"We shall die, then," he answered, with a bright smile. "And now, Captain Meadows, I must bid you adieu, thanking you for your kindness during the voyage, and you, too, good-by—you will command a ship of your own before the year is out. I trust, Mr. West, that I may see you again before I leave this part of the country. Farewell!"

He raised his red fez, inclined his noble head with the stately grace which characterized all his actions, and strode away in the direction from which he had come.

"Let me congratulate you, Mr. Hawkins," said the captain to the mate, as we walked homewards. "You are to command your own ship within the year."

"No such luck," the mate answered, with a pleased smile upon his mahogany face; "still there's no saying how things may come out. What d'ye think of him, Mr. West!"

"Why," said I, "I am very much interested in him. What a magnificent head and bearing he has for a young man. I suppose he cannot be more than thirty."

"Forty," said the mate.

"Sixty, if he is a day," remarked Captain Meadows. "Why, I have heard him talk quite familiarly of the first Afghan war. He was a man then, and that is close on forty years ago."

"Wonderful!" I ejaculated. "His skin is as smooth and his eyes are as clear as mine are. He is the superior priest of the three, no doubt."

"The inferior," said the captain, confidently. "That is why he does all the talking for them. Their minds are too elevated to descend to mere worldly chatter."

"They are the strangest pieces of flotsam and jetsam that ever was thrown upon this coast," I remarked. "My father will be mightily interested in them."

Indeed, I think the less you have to do with them the better for you," said the mate. "If I do command my own ship I'll promise you that I never carry live stock of that sort on board of her. But here we are all aboard and the anchor tripped, so we must bid you good-by."

The wagonette had just finished loading up when we arrived, and the chief places, on either side of the driver, had been reserved for my two companions, who speedily sprang into them. With a chorus of cheers the good fellows whirled away down the road, while my father, Esther and I stood upon the lawn and waved our hands to them until they disappeared behind the Cloomber woods, *en route* for the Wigtown railway station. Bark and crew had both vanished now from our little world, the only relic of either being the heaps of *débris* upon the beach, which were to lie there until the arrival of an agent from Lloyd's.

CHAPTER XIII

IN WHICH I SEE THAT WHICH HAS BEEN SEEN BY FEW

AT dinner that evening I mentioned to my father the episode of the three Buddhist priests, and found, as I had expected, that he was very much interested by my account of them. When, however, he heard of the high manner in which Ram Singh had spoken of him, and the distinguished position which he had assigned him among philologists, he became so excited that it was all we could do to prevent him from setting off then and there to make his acquaintance. Esther and I were relieved and glad when we at last succeeded in abstracting his boots and maneuvering him to his bedroom, for the exciting events of the last twenty-four hours had been too much for his weak frame and delicate nerves.

I was sitting at the open porch in the gloaming, turning over in my mind the unexpected events which had occurred so rapidly—the gale, the wreck, the rescue, and the strange character of the castaways—when my sister came quietly over to me and put her hand in mine.

"Don't you think, Jack," she said, in her low, sweet voice, "that we are forgetting our friends over at Cloomber? Hasn't all this excitement driven their fears and their danger out of our heads?"

"Out of our heads, but never out of our hearts," said I, laughing. "However, you are right, little one, for our attention has certainly been distracted from them. I shall walk up in the morning and see if I can see anything of them. By the way, tomorrow is the fateful 5th of October—one more day and all will be well with us."

"Or ill," said my sister, gloomily.

"Why, what a little croaker you are, to be sure!" I cried. "What in the world is coming over you?"

"I feel nervous and low-spirited," she answered, drawing closer to my side and shivering. "I feel as if some great peril were hanging over the heads of those we love. Why should these strange men wish to stay upon the coast?"

"What, the Buddhists?" I said, lightly. "Oh, these fellows have continual feast days and religious rites of all sorts. They have some very good reason for staying, you may be sure."

"Don't you think," said Esther, in an awestruck whisper, "that it is very strange that these priests should arrive here all the way from India just at the present moment? Have you not gathered from all you have heard that the general's fears in some way connected with India and the Indians?"

The remark made me thoughtful. "Why, now that you mention it," I answered, "I have some vague impression that the mystery is connected with some incident which occurred in that country. I am sure, however, that your fears would vanish if you saw Ram Singh. He is the very personification of wisdom and benevolence. He was shocked at the idea of our killing a sheep, or even a fish for his benefit—said he would rather die than have a hand in taking the life of an animal."

"It is very foolish of me to be so nervous," said my sister, bravely. "But you must promise me one thing, Jack. You will go up to Cloomber in the morning, and if you can see any of them you must tell them of these strange neighbors of ours. They are better able to judge than we are whether their presence has any significance or not."

"All right, little one," I answered, as we went indoors. "You have been over-excited by all these wild doings, and you need a sound night's rest to compose you. I'll do what you suggest, however, and our friends shall judge for themselves whether these poor devils should be sent about their business or not."

I made the promise to allay my sister's apprehensions, but in the bright sunlight of morning it appeared little less than absurd to imagine that our poor, vegetarian castaways could have any sinister intentions, or that their advent could have any effect upon the tenant of Cloomber. I was anxious myself, however, to see whether I could see anything of the Heatherstones, so after breakfast I walked up to the Hall. In their seclusion it was impossible for them to have learned anything of the recent events. I felt, therefore, that even if I should meet the general he could hardly regard me as an intruder while I had so much news to communicate.

The place had the same dreary and melancholy appearance which always characterized it. Looking through between the thick iron bars of the main gateway there was nothing to be seen of any of the occupants. One of the great Scotch firs had been blown down in the gale, and its long, ruddy trunk lay right across the grass-grown avenue; but no attempt had been made to remove it. Everything about the property had the same air of desolation and neglect, with the solitary exception of the massive and impenetrable fencing, which presented as unbroken and formidable an obstacle as ever to the would-be trespasser.

I walked round this barrier as far as our old trysting-place without finding any flaw through which I could get a glimpse of the house, for the fence had been erected with each rail overlapping the last, so as to secure absolute privacy for those inside. At the old spot, however, where I had had the memorable interview with the general on the occasion when he surprised me with his daughter, I found that the two loose rails had been refixed in such a manner that there was a gap of two inches or more between them. Through this I had a view of the house and of part of the lawn in front of it, and though I could see no signs of life outside or at any of the windows, I settled down with the intention of sticking to my post until I had a chance of speaking to one or other of the inmates. Indeed, the cold, dead aspect of the house had struck such a chill into my heart that I determined to scale the fence at whatever risk of incurring the general's displeasure rather than return without news of the Heatherstones.

Happily there was no need of this extreme expedient, for I had not been there half-an-hour before I heard the harsh sound of an opening lock, and the general himself emerged from the main door. To my surprise he was dressed in a military uniform—and that not the uniform in ordinary use in the British army. The red coat was strangely cut and stained with the weather. The trousers had originally been white, but had now faded to a dirty yellow. With a red sash across his chest and a straight sword hanging from his side he stood the living example of a by-gone type—the John Company's officer of forty years ago. He was followed by the ex-tramp, Corporal Rufus Smith, now well clad and prosperous, who limped along beside his master, the two pacing up and down the lawn absorbed in conversation. I observed that from time to time one or other of them would pause and glance furtively all about them, as though guarding keenly against a surprise.

I should have preferred communicating with the general alone, but since there was no dissociating him from his companion, I beat loudly on the fencing with my stick to attract their attention. They both faced round in a moment, and I could see from their gestures that they were disturbed and alarmed. I then elevated my stick above the barrier to show them where the sound proceeded from. At this the general began to walk in my direction with the air of a man who is bracing himself for an effort, but the other caught him by the wrist and endeavored to dissuade him. It was only when I shouted out my name and assured them that I was alone that I could prevail upon them to approach. Once assured of my identity the general ran eagerly towards me and greeted me with the utmost cordiality.

"This is truly kind of you, West," he said. "It is only at such times as these that one can judge who is a friend and who not. It would not be fair to you to ask you to come inside or to stay any time, but I am none the less very glad to see you."

"I have been anxious about you all," I said; "for it is some little time since I have seen or heard from any of you. How have you all been keeping?"

"Why, as well as could be expected. But we will be better to-morrow—we will be different men to-morrow, eh, corporal?"

"Yes, sir," said the corporal, raising his hand to his forehead in a military salute. "We'll be right as the bank to-morrow."

"The corporal and I are a little disturbed in our minds just now," the general explained, "but I have no doubt that all will come right. After all, there is nothing higher than Providence, and we are all in its hands. And how have you been, eh?"

"We have been very busy for one thing," said I. "I suppose you have heard nothing of the great shipwreck?"

"Not a word," the general answered, listlessly.

"I thought the noise of the wind would prevent you hearing the signal guns. She came ashore in the bay the night before last—a great bark from India."

"From India!" ejaculated the general.

"Yes. Her crew were saved, fortunately, and have all been sent on to Glasgow."

"All sent on!" cried the general, with a face as bloodless as a corpse.

"All except three rather strange characters who claim to be Buddhist priests. They have decided to remain for a few days upon the coast."

The words were hardly out of my mouth when the general dropped upon his knees with his long, thin arms extended to heaven. "Thy will be done!" he cried in a crackling voice. "Thy blessed will be done!" I could see through the crack that Corporal Rufus Smith's face had turned to a sickly yellow shade, and that he was wiping the perspiration from his brow.

"It's like my luck!" he said. "After all these years, to come just when I have got a snug billet."

"Never mind, my lad," the general said, rising and squaring his shoulders like a man who braces himself for an effort. "Be it what it may we'll face it as British soldiers should. D'ye remember at Chillianwallah, when you had to run from your guns to our square, and the Sikh horse came thundering down on our bayonets? We didn't flinch then, and we won't flinch now. It seems to me that I feel better than I have done for years. It was the uncertainty that was killing me."

"And the infernal jingle-jangle," said the corporal. "Well, we all go together—that's some consolation."

"Good-bye, West," said the general. "Be a good husband to Gabriel, and give my poor wife a home. I don't think she will trouble you long. Good-bye! God bless you!"

"Look here, general," I said, peremptorily, breaking off a piece of wood to make communication more easy, "this sort of thing has been going on too long. What are these hints and allusions and innuendoes? It is time we had a little plain speaking. What is it you fear? Out with it! Are you in dread of these Hindoos? If you are I am able, on my father's authority, to have them arrested as rogues and vagabonds."

"No, no, that would never do," he answered, shaking his head. "You will learn about the wretched business soon enough. Mordaunt knows where to lay his hand upon the papers bearing on the matter. You can consult him about it to-morrow."

"But surely," I cried, "if the peril is so imminent something may be done to avert it. If you would but tell me what you fear I should know how to act."

"My dear friend," he said, "there is nothing to be done, so calm yourself; and let things take their course. It has been folly on my part to shelter myself behind mere barriers of wood and stone. The fact is, that inaction was terrible to me, and I felt that to do anything, however futile, in the nature of a precaution, was better than passive resignation. My humble friend here and I have placed ourselves in a position in which, I trust, no poor fellow will ever find himself again. We can only recommend ourselves to the unfailing goodness of the Almighty, and trust that what we have endured in this world may lessen our atonement in the world to come. I must leave you now, for I have many papers to destroy and much to arrange. Good-bye." He pushed his hand through the hole which I had made and grasped mine in a solemn farewell, after which he walked back to the Hall with a firm and decided step, still followed by the crippled corporal.

I walked back to Branksome much disturbed by this interview, and extremely puzzled as to what course I should pursue. It was evident now that my sister's suspicions were correct, and that there was some very intimate connection between the presence of the three Orientals and the mysterious peril which hung over the towers of Cloomber. It was difficult for me to associate the noble-faced Ram Singh's gentle, refined manner and words of wisdom with any deed of violence; yet now that I thought of it I could see that a terrible capacity for wrath lay behind his shaggy brows and dark, piercing eyes. I felt that of all men whom I had ever met he was the one whose displeasure I should least care to face. But how could two men so widely dissociated as the foul-mouthed old corporal of artillery and the distinguished Anglo-Indian general have each earned the ill-will of these strange castaways? And if the danger was a positive, physical one, why should he not consent to my proposal to have the three men placed under custody? though I confess it would have gone much against my grain to act in so inhospitable a manner upon such vague and shadowy grounds. These questions were absolutely unanswerable; and yet the solemn words and the terrible gravity which I had seen in the faces of both the old soldiers forbade me from thinking that their fears were entirely unfounded. It was all a puzzle—an absolutely insoluble puzzle. One thing at least was clear to me—and that was that in the present state of my knowledge, and after the general's distinct prohibition, it was impossible for me to interfere in any way. I could only wait and pray that, whatever the danger might be, it might pass over, or at least that my dear Gabriel and her brother might be protected against it.

I was walking down the lane lost in thought, and had got as far as the wicket gate which opens upon the Branksome lawn, when I was surprised to hear my father's voice raised in most animated and excited converse. The old man had been of late so abstracted from the daily affairs of the world, and so absorbed in his own special studies, that it was difficult to engage his attention upon any ordinary mundane topic. Curious to know what it was that had drawn him so far out of himself, I opened the gate softly, and walking quietly round the laurel bushes, found him sitting, to my astonishment, with none other than the very man who was occupying my thoughts, Ram Singh, the Buddhist. The two were sitting upon a garden bench, and the Oriental appeared to be laying down some weighty proposition, checking every point upon his long, quivering, brown fingers, while my father, with his hands thrown abroad and his face awry, was loud in protestation and in argument. So absorbed were they in their controversy that I stood within a hand-touch of them for a minute or more before they became conscious of my presence. On observing me the priest sprang to his feet and greeted me with the same lofty courtesy and dignified grace which had so impressed me the day before.

"I promised myself yesterday," he said, "the pleasure of calling upon your father. You see I have kept my word. I have even been daring enough to question his views upon some points in connection with the Sanscrit and Hindoo tongues, with the result that we have been arguing for an hour or more without either of us convincing the other. Without pretending to as deep a theoretical knowledge as that which has made the name of James Hunter West a household word among Oriental scholars, I happen to have given considerable attention to this one point, and indeed I am in a position to say that I *know* his views to be unsound. I assure you, sir, that up to the year 700, or even later, Sanscrit was the ordinary language of the great bulk of the inhabitants of India."

"And I assure you, sir," said my father warmly, "that it was dead and forgotten at that date, save by the learned who used it as a vehicle for scientific and religious works—just as Latin was used in the middle ages long after it had ceased to be spoken by any European nation."

"If you will consult the puranas you will find," said Ram Singh, "that this theory, though commonly received, is entirely untenable."

"And if you will consult the Ramayana, and more particularly the canonical books on Buddhist discipline," cried my father, "you will find that the theory is unassailable."

"But look at the Kullavagga," said our visitor, earnestly.

"And look at King Asoka," shouted my father, triumphantly. "When, in the year 300 before the Christian era—*before*, mind you—he ordered the laws of Buddha to be engraved upon the rocks, what language did he employ, eh? Was it Sanscrit?—no! And why was it not Sanscrit? Because the lower orders of his subjects would not have been able to understand a word of it. Ha! ha! That was the reason. How are you going to get round King Asoka's edict, eh?"

"He carved them in the various dialects," Ram Singh answered. "But energy is too precious a thing to be wasted in mere wind in this style. The sun has passed its meridian, and I must return to my companions."

"I am sorry that you have not brought them to see us," said my father, courteously. He was, I could see, uneasy lest in the eagerness of debate he had overstepped the bounds of hospitality.

"They do not mix with the world," Ram Singh answered, rising to his feet. "They are of a higher grade than I, and more sensitive to contaminating influences. They are immersed in a six months' meditation upon the mystery of the third incarnation, which has lasted from the time that we left the Himalayas. I shall not see you again, Mr. Hunter West, and I therefore bid you farewell. Your old age will be a happy one, as it deserves to be, and your Eastern studies will have a lasting effect upon the knowledge and literature of your own country. Farewell!"

"And am I also to see no more of you?" I asked.

"Unless you will walk with me along the seashore," he answered. "But you have already been out this morning, and may be tired. I ask too much of you."

"Nay, I should be delighted to come," I responded from my heart, and we set off together, accompanied for some little distance by my father, who would gladly, I could see, have reopened the Sanscrit controversy, had not his stock of breath been too limited to allow of his talking and walking at the same time.

"He is a learned man," Ram Singh remarked, after we had left him behind; "but, like many another, he is intolerant towards opinions which differ from his own. He will know better some day."

I made no answer to this observation, and we trudged along for a time in silence, keeping well down to the water's edge, where the sands afforded a good foothold. The sand dunes which lined the coast formed a continuous ridge upon our left, cutting us off entirely from all human observation, while on the right the broad Channel stretched away with hardly a sail to break its silvery uniformity. The Buddhist priest and I were absolutely alone with Nature. I could not help reflecting that if he were really the dangerous man that the mate affected to consider him, or that might be inferred from the words of General Heatherstone, I had placed myself completely in his power. Yet such was the majestic benignity of the man's aspect, and the unruffled serenity of his deep, dark eyes, that I could afford in his presence to let fear and suspicion blow past me as lightly as the breeze which whistled round us. His face might be stern, and even terrible, but I felt that he could never be unjust. As I glanced from time to time at his noble profile and the sweep of his jet-black beard, his rough-spun tweed travelling suit struck me with an almost painful sense of incongruity, and I re-clothed him in my imagination with the grand, sweeping Oriental costume which is the fitting and proper frame for such a picture— the only garb which does not detract from the dignity and grace of the wearer. The place to which he led me was a small fisher cottage which had been deserted some years before by its tenant, but still stood gaunt and bare, with the thatch partly blown away and the windows and door in sad disrepair. This dwelling, which the poorest Scotch beggar would have shrunk from, was the one which these singular men had preferred to the proffered hospitality of the laird's house. A small garden, now a mass of tangled brambles, stood round it, and through this my acquaintance picked his way to the ruined door. He glanced into the house and then waved his hand for me to follow him.

"You have now an opportunity," he said, in a subdued, reverential voice, "of seeing a spectacle which few Europeans have had the privilege of beholding. Inside that cottage you will find two Yogis—men who are only one remove from the highest plane of adeptship. They are both wrapped in an ecstatic trance, otherwise I should not venture to obtrude your presence upon them. Their astral bodies have departed from them, to be present at the feast of lamps in the holy lamastery of Rudok in Thibet. Tread lightly, lest by stimulating their corporeal functions you recall them before their devotions are completed."

Walking slowly and on tiptoe, I picked my way through the weed-grown garden, and peered through the open doorway. There was no furniture in the dreary interior, nor anything to cover the uneven floor save a litter of fresh straw in a corner.

Among this straw two men were crouching, the one small and wizened, the other large-boned and gaunt, with their legs crossed in Oriental fashion and their heads sunk upon their breasts. Neither of them looked up, or took the smallest notice of our presence. They were so still and silent that they might have been two bronze statues but for the slow and measured rhythm of their breathing. Their faces, however, had a peculiar, ashen grey color, very different from the healthy brown of my companion's; and I observed, on stooping my head, that only the whites of their eyes were visible, the balls being turned upwards beneath the lids. In front of them upon a small mat lay an earthernware pitcher of water and half a loaf of bread, together with a sheet of paper inscribed with certain cabalistic characters. Ram Singh glanced at these, and then, motioning to me to withdraw, followed me out into the garden.

"I am not to disturb them until ten o'clock," he said. "You have now seen in operation one of the grandest results of our occult philosophy, the dissociation of spirit from body. Not only are the spirits of these holy men standing at the present moment by the banks of the Ganges, but those spirits are clothed in a material covering so identical with their real bodies that none of the faithful will ever doubt that Lal Hoomi and Mowdar Khan are actually among them. This is accomplished by our power of resolving an object into its chemical atoms, of conveying these atoms with a speed which exceeds that of lightning to any given spot, and of there re-precipitating them and compelling them to retake their original form. Of old it was necessary to convey the whole body in this way, but we have since found that it was as easy and more convenient to transmit material enough merely to build up an outside shell or semblance of a body. This we have termed the astral body."

"But if you can transmit your spirits so readily," I observed, "why should they be accompanied by any body at all?"

"In communicating with brother initiates we are able to employ our spirits only; but when we wish to come in contact with ordinary mankind it is essential that we should appear in some form which they can see and comprehend."

"You have interested me deeply in all that you have told me,"
I said, grasping the hand which Ram Singh had held out to me
as a sign that our interview was at an end. "I shall often think of
our short acquaintance."

"You will derive much benefit from it," he said, slowly, still
holding my hand and looking gravely and sadly into my eyes. "You
must remember that what will happen in the future is not necessarily bad because it does not fall in with your preconceived ideas
of right. Be not hasty in your judgments. There are certain great
rules which must be carried out, at whatever cost to individuals.
Their operation may appear to you to be harsh and cruel, but that
is as nothing compared to the dangerous precedent which would
be established by not enforcing them. The ox and the sheep are
safe from us, but the man with the blood of the highest upon his
hands should not and shall not live."

He threw up his arms at the last words with a fierce, threaten-
ing gesture, and turning away from me strode back to the ruined
hut. I stood gazing after him until he disappeared through the
doorway, and then started off for home, revolving in my mind all
that I had heard, and more particularly this last outburst of the
occult philosopher. Far on the right I could see the tall, white
tower of Cloomber standing out clear-cut and sharp against a
dark cloud-bank which rose behind it. I thought how any travel-
ler who chanced to pass that way would envy in his heart the
tenant of that magnificent building, and how little they would
guess the strange terrors, the nameless dangers, which were
gathering about his head. The black cloud-wrack was but the
image, I reflected, of the darker, more sombre, storm which was
about to burst.

"Whatever it all means, and however it happens," I ejaculated, "God grant that the innocent be not confounded with the
guilty."

My father, when I reached home, was still in a ferment over
his learned disputation with the stranger. "I trust, Jack," he said,
"that I did not handle him too roughly. I should remember that
I am *in loco magistri*, and be less prone to argue with my guests.
Yet, when he took up this most untenable position, I could not
refrain from attacking him and hurling him out of it, which

indeed I did, though you, who are ignorant of the niceties of the question, may have failed to perceive it. You observed, however, that my reference to King Asoka's edicts was so conclusive that he rose and took his leave."

"You held your own bravely," I answered; "but what is your impression of the man now that you have seen him?"

"Why," said my father, "he is one of those holy men who, under the various names of Sannasis, Yogis, Sevras, Qualanders, Hakims, and Cufis, have devoted their lives to the study of the mysteries of the Buddhist faith. He is, I take it, a theosophist, or worshipper of the God of knowledge, the highest grade of which is the adept. This man and his companions have not attained this high position or they could not have crossed the sea without contamination. It is probable that they are all advanced chelas who hope in time to attain to the supreme honor of adeptship."

"But, father," interrupted my sister, "this does not explain why men of such sanctity and attainments should choose to take up their quarters on the shores of a desolate Scotch bay."

"Ah, there you get beyond me," my father answered. "I may suggest, however, that it is nobody's business but their own, as long as they keep the peace and are amenable to the law of the land."

"Have you ever heard," I asked, "that these higher priests of whom you speak have powers which are unknown to us?"

"Why, Eastern literature is full of it. The Bible is an Eastern book, and is it not full of the record of such powers from cover to cover? It is unquestionable that they have in the past known many of Nature's secrets which are lost to us. I cannot say, however, that the modern theosophists really possess the powers that they claim."

"Are they a vindictive class of people? I asked. "Is there any offense among them which can only be expiated by death?"

"Not that I know of," my father answered, raising his white eyebrows in surprise. "You appear to be in an inquisitive humor this afternoon—what is the object of all these questions? Have our Eastern neighbors aroused your curiosity or suspicion in any way?

I parried the question as best I might, for I was unwilling to let the old man know what was in my mind. No good purpose could come from his enlightenment; his age and his health demanded rest rather than anxiety; and indeed with the best will in the world I should have found it difficult to explain to another what was so very obscure to myself. For every reason I felt that it was best that he should be kept in the dark.

Never in all my experience have I known a day pass so slowly as did that eventful 5th of October. In every possible manner I endeavored to while away the tedious hours, and yet it seemed as if darkness would never arrive. I tried to read, I tried to write, I paced about the lawn, I walked to the end of the lane, I put new flies upon my fishing-hooks, I began to index my father's library—in a dozen ways I endeavored to relieve the suspense which was becoming intolerable. My sister, I could see, was suffering from the same feverish restlessness. Again and again our good father remonstrated with us in his mild way for our erratic behavior and the continual interruption of his work which arose from it. At last, however, the tea was brought, and the tea was taken, the curtains were drawn, the lamps lit, and after another interminable interval the prayers were read and the servants dismissed to their rooms. My father compounded and swallowed his nightly jorum of toddy, and then shuffled off to his room, leaving the two of us in the parlor with our nerves in a tingle and our minds full of the most vague and yet terrible apprehensions.

CHAPTER XIV

OF THE VISITOR WHO RAN DOWN THE ROAD IN THE NIGHT-TIME

It was a quarter past ten o'clock by the parlor time-piece when my father went off to his room, and left Esther and myself together. We heard his slow steps dying away up the creaking staircase, until the distant slamming of a door announced that he had reached his sanctum. The simple oil lamp upon the table threw a weird, uncertain light over the old room, flickering upon the carved oak panelling, and casting strange, fantastic shadows from the high-elbowed, straight-backed furniture. My sister's white, anxious face stood out in the obscurity with a startling exactness of profile, like one of Rembrandt's portraits. We sat opposite to each other on either side of the table, with no sound breaking the silence save the measured ticking of the clock and the intermittent chirping of a cricket beneath the grate. There was something awe-inspiring in the absolute stillness. The whistling of a belated peasant upon the high road was a relief to us, and we strained our ears to catch the last of his notes as he plodded steadily homewards.

At first we had made some pretense—she of knitting and I of reading; but we soon abandoned the useless deception, and sat uneasily waiting, starting and glancing at each other with questioning eyes whenever the fagot crackled in the fire or a rat scampered behind the wainscot. There was a heavy, electrical feeling in the air, which weighed us down with a foreboding of disaster. I rose and flung the hall door open to admit the fresh breeze of the night. Ragged clouds swept across the sky, and the moon peeped out at times between their hurrying fringes, bathing the whole country-side in its cold, white radiance. From where I stood in the doorway I could see the edge of the Cloomber wood, though the house itself was only visible from the rising ground some little distance off. At my sister's suggestion we walked together, she with her shawl over her head, as far as the summit of this elevation, and looked out in the direction of the Hall. There was no illumination of the windows to-night. From roof to basement not a light twinkled in any part of the great building. Its huge mass loomed up dark and sullen amid the trees which surrounded it, looking more like some giant sarcophagus than a human habitation. To our overwrought nerves there was something of terror in its mere bulk and its silence. We stood for some little time peering at it through the darkness, and then we made our way back to the parlor again, where we sat waiting—waiting, we knew not for what, and yet with the absolute conviction that some terrible experience was in store for us.

It was twelve o'clock or close on to it when my sister suddenly sprang to her feet and held up her finger to bespeak attention. "Do you hear nothing?" she asked.

I strained my ears, but without success.

"Come to the door," she cried, with a trembling voice. "Now can you hear anything?"

In the deep silence of the night I distinctly heard a dull, murmuring, clattering sound, continuous apparently, but very faint and low. "What is it?" I asked in a subdued voice.

"It's the sound of a man running towards us," she answered; and then, suddenly dropping the last semblance of self-command, she fell upon her knees beside the table and began praying aloud with that frenzied earnestness which intense, overpowering fear can produce, breaking off now and again into half-hysterical whimperings.

I could distinguish the sound clearly enough now to know that her quick, feminine perception had not deceived her, and that it was indeed caused by a running man. On he came, and on down the high road, his footfalls ringing out clearer and sharper every moment. An urgent messenger he must be, for he neither paused nor slackened his pace. The quick, crisp rattle was changed suddenly to a dull, muffled murmur. He had reached the point where sand had been recently laid down for a hundred yards or so. In a few moments, however, he was back on hard ground again and his flying feet were nearer and ever nearer. He must, I reflected, be abreast of the head of the lane now. Would he hold on? or would he turn down to Branksome? The thought had hardly crossed my mind when I heard by the difference of the sound that the runner had turned the corner, and that his goal was beyond all question the laird's house. Rushing down to the gate of the lawn, I reached it just as our visitor dashed it open and fell into my arms. I could see in the moonlight that it was none other than Mordaunt Heatherstone.

"My God!" I cried, "what has happened? What is amiss, Mordaunt?"

"My father!" he gasped—"my father!" His hat was gone, his eyes dilated with terror, and his face as bloodless as that of a corpse. I could feel that the hands which clasped my arms were quivering and shaking with emotion.

"You are exhausted," I said, leading him into the parlor. "Give yourself a moment's rest before you speak to us. Be calm, man, you are with your best friends." I laid him on the old horsehair sofa, while Esther, whose fears had all flown to the winds now that something practical was to be done, dashed some brandy into a tumbler and brought it to him. The stimulant had a marvellous effect upon him, for the color began to come back into his pale cheeks and the light of recognition in his eyes. He sat up and took Esther's hand in both of his, like a man who is waking out of some bad dream and wishes to assure himself that he is really in safety.

"Your father?" I asked. "What of him?"

"He is gone."

"Gone!"

"Yes, he is gone; and so is Corporal Rufus Smith. We shall never set eyes upon them again."

"But where have they gone?" I cried. "This is unworthy of you, Mordaunt. What right have we to sit here, allowing our private feelings to overcome us, while there is a possibility of succoring your father? Up, man! Let us follow him. Tell me only what direction he took."

"It's no use," young Heatherstone answered, burying his face in his hands. "Don't reproach me, West, for you don't know all the circumstances. What can we do to reverse the tremendous and unknown laws which are acting against us? The blow has long been hanging over us, and now it has fallen. God help us!"

"In heaven's name tell me what has happened?" said I, excitedly. "We must not yield to despair."

"We can do nothing until daybreak," he answered. "We shall then endeavor to obtain some trace of them. It is hopeless at present."

"And how about Gabriel and Mrs. Heatherstone?" I asked. "Can we not bring them down from the Hall at once? Your poor sister must be distracted with terror."

"She knows nothing of it," Mordaunt answered. "She sleeps at the other side of the house, and has not heard or seen anything. As to my poor mother, she has expected some such event for so long a time that it has not come upon her as a surprise. She is, of course, overwhelmed with grief, but would, I think, prefer to be left to herself for the present. Her firmness and composure should be a lesson to me; but I am constitutionally excitable, and this catastrophe coming after our long period of suspense deprived me of my very reason for a time."

"If we can do nothing until morning," I said, "you have time to tell us all that has occurred."

"I shall do so," he answered, rising and holding his shaking hands to the fire. "You know already that we have had reason for some time—for many years, in fact—to fear that a terrible retribution was hanging over my father's head for a certain action of his early life. In this action he was associated with the man known as Corporal Rufus Smith; so that the fact of the latter finding his way to my father was a warning to us that the time had come, and that this 5th of October—the anniversary of the misdeed—would be the day of its atonement. I told you of our fears in my letter; and if I am not mistaken, my father also had some conversation with you, West, upon the subject. When I saw yesterday morning that he had hunted out the old uniform which he has always retained since he wore it in the Afghan war,

I was sure that the end was at hand, and that our forebodings would be realized.

"He appeared to be more composed in the afternoon than I have seen him for years, and spoke freely of his life in India and of the incidents of his youth. About nine o'clock he requested us to go to our own rooms, and locked us in there—a precaution which he frequently took when the dark fit was upon him. It was always his endeavor, poor soul, to keep us clear of the curse which had fallen upon his own unfortunate head. Before parting from us he tenderly embraced my mother and Gabriel, and he afterwards followed me to my room, where he clasped my hand affectionately and gave into my charge a small packet addressed to yourself."

"To me?" I interrupted.

"To you. I shall fulfill my commission whenever I have told you my story. I conjured him to allow me to sit up with him and to share any danger which might arise; but he implored me with irresistible earnestness not to add to his troubles by thwarting his arrangements. Seeing that I was really distressing him by my pertinacity, I at last allowed him to close the door and to turn the key upon the outside. I shall always reproach myself for my want of firmness. But what can you do when your own father refuses your assistance or co-operation? You cannot force yourself upon him."

"I am sure that you did all you could do," my sister said.

"I meant to, dear Esther, but God help me, it was hard to tell what was right. He left me, and I heard his footsteps die away down the long corridor. It was then about ten o'clock, or a little after. For a time I paced up and down the room, and then carrying the lamp to the head of my bed, I lay upon it without undressing, reading 'St. Thomas à Kempis,' and praying from my heart that the night might pass safely over us. I had at last fallen into a troubled sleep when I was suddenly aroused by a loud, sonorous sound ringing in my ears. I sat up bewildered, but all was silent again. The lamp was burning low, and my watch showed me that it was going on to midnight. I blundered to my feet, and was striking a match with the intention of lighting the candles, when the sharp, vehement cry broke out again so loud and so clear that it might have been in the very room with me. My chamber is in the front of the house, while those of my mother and sister are at the back, so that I am the only one who commands a view of the avenue. Rushing to the window I drew the blind aside and looked out. You know that the gravel drive opens up so as to form a broad stretch immediately in front of the house. Just in the centre of this clear space there stood three men looking up at the house. The moon shone full upon them, glistening on their upturned eyeballs, and by its light I could see that they were swarthy-faced and black-haired, of a type that I was familiar with among the Sikhs and Afreedees. Two of them were thin, with eager, aesthetic countenances, while the third was kinglike and majestic, with a noble figure and flowing beard."

"Ram Singh!" I ejaculated.

"What, you know them," exclaimed Mordaunt, in great surprise. "You have met them?"

"I know of them. They are Buddhist priests," I answered; "but go on."

"They stood in a line," he continued, "sweeping their arms upwards and downwards, while their lips moved as if repeating some prayer or incantation. Suddenly they ceased to gesticulate, and broke out for the third time into the wild, weird, piercing cry which had roused me from my slumber. Never shall I forget that shrill, dreadful summons, swelling and reverberating through the silent night with an intensity of sound which is still ringing in my ears. As it died slowly away there was a rasping and creaking as of keys and bolts, followed by the clang of an opening door and the clatter of hurrying feet. From my window I saw my father and Corporal Rufus Smith rush frantically out of the house, hatless and unkempt, like men who are obeying a sudden and overpowering impulse. The three strangers laid no hands upon them, but the whole five swept swiftly away down the avenue and vanished among the trees. I am positive that no force was used, or constraint of any visible kind, and yet I am as sure that my poor father and his companion were helpless prisoners as if I had seen them dragged away in manacles. All this took little time in the acting. From the first summons which disturbed my sleep to the last shadowy glimpse which I had of them between the tree trunks could hardly have occupied more than five minutes of actual time. So sudden was it, and so strange, that when the drama was over and they were gone, I could have believed that it was all some terrible nightmare, some delusion, had I not felt that the impression was too real, too vivid to be imputed to fancy. I threw my whole weight against my bedroom door in the hope of forcing the lock. It stood firm for a while, but I flung myself upon it again and again, until something snapped and I found myself in the passage. My first thought was for my mother. I rushed to her room and turned the key in her door. The moment that I did so she stepped out into the corridor in her dressing-gown, and held up a warning finger.

" 'No noise,' she said. 'Gabriel is asleep. They have been called away?'

" 'They have,' I answered.

" 'God's will be done!' she cried. 'Your poor father will be happier in the next world than he has ever been in this. Thank heaven that Gabriel is asleep. I gave her chloral in her cocoa.'

" 'What am I to do?' I said, distractedly. 'Where have they gone? How can I help him? We cannot let him go from us like this, or leave these men to do what they will with him. Shall I ride into Wigtown and rouse the police?'

" 'Anything rather than that,' my mother said, earnestly. 'He has begged me again and again to avoid it. My son, we shall never set eyes on your father again. You may marvel at my dry eyes; but if you knew as I know the peace which death would bring him, you could not find it in your heart to mourn for him. All pursuit is, I feel, vain; and yet some pursuit there must be. Let it be as private as possible. We cannot serve him better than by consulting his wishes.'

" 'But every minute is precious,' I cried. 'Even now he may be calling upon as to rescue him from the clutches of these dark-skinned fiends.'

The thought so maddened me that I rushed out of the house and down to the high road, but once there I had no indication in which direction to turn. The whole wide moor lay before me, without a sign of movement upon its broad expanse. I listened, but not a sound broke the perfect stillness of the night. It was then, my dear friends, as I stood, not knowing in which direction to turn, that the horror and responsibility broke full upon me. I felt that I was combating against forces of which I knew nothing. All was strange and dark and terrible. The thought of you, and of the help which I might look for from your advice and assistance, was a beacon of hope to me. At Branksome, at least, I should receive sympathy, and, above all, directions as to what I should do; for my mind is in such a whirl that I cannot trust my own judgment. My mother was content to be alone, my sister asleep, and no prospect of being able to do anything until daybreak. Under those circumstances what more natural than that I should fly to you as fast as my feet would carry me? You have a clear head, Jack; speak out, man, and tell me what I should do. Esther, what should I do?" He turned from one to the other of us with outstretched hands and eager, questioning eyes.

"You can do nothing while the darkness lasts," I answered. "We must report the matter to the Wigtown police; but we need not send our message to them until we are actually starting upon the search, so as to comply with the law and yet have a private investigation, as your mother wishes. John Fullarton, over the hill, has a lurcher dog which is as good as a bloodhound. If we set him on the general's trail he will run him down if he has to follow him to John o' Groats."

"It is terrible to wait calmly here while he may need our assistance."

"I fear our assistance could under any circumstances do him little good. There are forces at work here which are beyond human intervention. Besides, there is no alternative. We have, apparently, no possible clue as to the direction which they have taken, and for us to wander aimlessly over the moor in the darkness would be to waste the strength which may be more profitably used in the morning. It will be daylight by five o'clock. In an hour or so we can walk over the hill together and get Fullarton's dog."

"Another hour!" Mordaunt groaned, "every minute seems an age."

"Lie down on the sofa again and rest yourself," said I. "You cannot serve your father better than by laying up all the strength you can, for we may have a weary trudge before us. But you mentioned a packet which the general had intended for me."

"It is here," he answered, drawing a small, flat parcel from his pocket and handing it over to me; "you will find, no doubt, that it will explain all which has been so mysterious."

The packet was sealed at either end with black wax, bearing the impress of the flying griffin, which I knew to be the general's crest. It was further secured by a band of broad tape which I cut with my pocket knife. Across the outside was written, in bold handwriting: "J Fothergill West, Esq.," and underneath, "To be handed to that gentleman in the event of the disappearance or decease of Major-General J. B. Heatherstone, V. C., C. B., late of the Indian Army." So at last I was to know the dark secret which had cast a shadow over our lives. Here in my hands I held the solution of it. With eager fingers I broke the seals and undid the wrapper. A note and a small bundle of discolored paper lay within. I drew the lamp over to me and opened the former. It was dated from the preceding afternoon, and ran in this way:

MY DEAR WEST,—I should have satisfied your very natural curiosity on the subject which we have had occasion to talk of more than once, but I refrained for your own sake. I knew by sad experience how unsettling and unnerving it is to be forever waiting for a catastrophe which you are convinced must befall, and which you can neither avert nor accelerate. Though it affects me specially, as being the person most concerned, I am still conscious that the natural sympathy which I have observed in you, and your regard for Gabriel's father, would both combine to render you unhappy if you knew the hopelessness and yet the vagueness of the fate which threatens me. I feared to disturb your mind, and I was, therefore, silent, though at some cost to myself, for my isolation has been not the least of the troubles which have weighed me down. Many signs, however, and chief among them the presence of the Buddhists upon the coast as described by you this morning, have convinced me that the weary waiting is at last over and that the hour of retribution is at hand. Why I should have been allowed to live nearly forty years after my offense, is more than I can understand, but it is possible that those who had command over my fate know that such a life is the greatest of all penalties to me. Never for an hour, night or day, have they suffered me to forget that they have marked me down as their victim. Their accursed astral bell has been ringing my knell for twoscore years, reminding me ever that there is no spot upon earth where I can hope to be in safety. Oh, the peace, the blessed peace of dissolution! Come what may on the other side of the tomb, I shall at least be quit of that thrice terrible sound.

There is no need for me to enter into the wretched business again, or to detail at any length the events of the fifth of October, 1841, and the various circumstances which led up to the death of Ghoolab Shah, the arch adept. I have torn a sheaf of leaves from my old journal, in which you will find a bald account of the matter, and an independent narrative was furnished by Sir Edward Elliott, of the Artillery, to the *Star of India* some years ago—in which, however, the names were suppressed. I have reason to believe that many people, even among those who knew India well, thought that Sir Edward was romancing, and that he had evolved his incidents from his imagination. The few faded leaves which I send you will show you that this is not the case, and that our men of science must recognize powers and laws which can and have been used by man, but which are unknown to European civilization.

I do not wish to whine or to whimper; but I cannot help feeling that I have had hard measure dealt me in this world. I would not, God knows, take the life of any man, far less an aged one, in cold blood. My temper and nature, however, were always fiery and headstrong, and in action when my blood is up I have no knowledge of what I am about. Neither the corporal or I would have laid a finger upon Ghoolab Shah had we not seen that the tribesmen were rallying behind him. Well, well; it is an old story now, and there is no profit in discussing it. May no other poor fellow ever have the same evil fortune!

I have written a short supplement to the statements contained in my journal for your information, and that of any one else who may chance to be interested in the matter. And now, adieu! Be a good husband to Gabriel; and if your sister be brave enough to marry into such a devil-ridden family as ours, by all means let her do so. I have left enough to keep my poor wife in comfort. When she rejoins me I should wish it to be equally divided between the children. If you hear that I am gone, do not pity, but congratulate

Your unfortunate friend,

JOHN BERTHIER HEATHERSTONE.

I threw aside the letter and picked up the roll of blue foolscap which contained the solution of the mystery. It was all ragged and frayed at the inner edge, with traces of gum and thread still adhering to it, to show that it had been torn out of a strongly bound volume. The ink with which it had been written had faded somewhat; but across the head of the first page was inscribed in bold, clear characters, evidently of later date than the rest, "Journal of Lieutenant J. B. Heatherstone, in the Thull valley during the autumn of 1841," and the underneath, "This extract contains some account of the events of the first week of October of that year, including the skirmish of the Terada ravine and the death of the man Ghoolab Shah." I have the narrative lying before me now, and I copy it verbatim. If it contains some matter which has not direct bearing upon the question at issue, I can only say that I thought it better to publish what is irrelevant than by cutting and clipping to lay the whole statement open to the charge of having been tampered with.

CHAPTER XV

THE DAY-BOOK OF JOHN BERTHIER HEATHERSTONE

THULL VALLEY, Oct. 1, 1841.—The Fifth Bengal and the Thirty-third Queen's passed through this morning on their way to the front. Had tiffin with the Bengalese. Latest news from home that two attempts had been made on the Queen's life by semi-maniacs named Francis and Bean.

It promises to be a hard winter. The snowline has descended a thousand feet upon the peaks, but the passes will be open for weeks to come, and even if they were blocked, we have established so many depôts in the country that Pollock and Nott will have no difficulty in holding their own. They shall not meet with the fate of Elphinstone's army. One such tragedy is enough for a century.

Elliott, of the Artillery, and I, are answerable for the safety of the communications for a distance of twenty miles or more, from the mouth of the valley to this side of the wooden bridge over the Lotar. Goodenough, of the rifles, is responsible on the other side; and Lieutenant-Colonel Sidney Herbert, of the Engineers, has a general supervision over both sections. Our force is not strong enough for the work which has to be done. I have a company and a half of our own regiment, and a squadron of Sowars, who are of no use at all among the rocks. Elliott has three guns, but several of his men are down with cholera, and I doubt if he has enough to serve more than two. [Note: capiscum for cholera—tried it.] On the other hand, each convoy is usually provided with some guard of its own, though it is often absurdly inefficient. These valleys and ravines which branch out of the main pass are alive with Afreedees and Pathans, who are keen robbers as well as religious fanatics. I wonder they don't swoop down on some of our caravans. They could plunder them and get back to their mountain fastnesses before we could interfere or overtake them. Nothing but fear will restrain them. If I had my way I would hang one at the mouth of every ravine as a warning to the gang. They are personifications of the devil to look at, hawk-nosed, full-lipped, with a mane of tangled hair, and most Satanic sneer. No news to-day from the front.

October 2.—I must really ask Herbert for another company at the very least. I am convinced that the communications would be cut off if any serious attack were made upon us. Now, this morning two urgent messages were sent me from two different points more than sixteen miles apart, to say that there were signs of a descent of the tribes. Elliott, with one gun and the Sowars, went to the further ravine, while I, with the infantry, hurried to the other; but we found it was a false alarm. I saw no signs of the hillmen, and though we were greeted by a sputter of jezail bullets we were unable to capture any of the rascals. Woe betide them if they fall into my hands! I would give them as short a shrift as ever a Highland cateran got from a Glasgow judge. These continued alarms may mean nothing or they may be an indication that the hillmen are assembling and have some plan in view.

We have had no news from the front for some time, but to-day a convoy of wounded came through with the intelligence that Nott had taken Ghuznee. I hope he warmed up any of the black rascals that fell into his hands. No word of Pollock. An elephant battery came up from the Punjaub, looking in a very good condition. There were several convalescents with it going up to rejoin their regiments. Knew none of them except Mostyn of the Hussars and young Blakesley, who was my fag at Charterhouse, and whom I have never seen since. Punch and cigars *al fresco* up to eleven o'clock. Letters to-day from Wills and Co., about their little bill forwarded on from Delhi. Thought a campaign freed a man from these annoyances. Wills says in his note that since his written applications have been in vain, he must call upon me in person. If he calls upon me now he will assuredly be the boldest and most persevering of tailors. A line from

Calcutta Daisy and another from Hobhouse to say that Matilda comes in for all the money under the will. I am glad of it.

October 3.—Glorious news from the front to-day. Barclay, of the Madras Cavalry, galloped through with dispatches. Pollock entered Cabul triumphantly on the 16th of last month, and, better still, Lady Sale has been rescued by Shakespeare, and brought safe into the British camp, together with the other hostages. *"Te Deum Laudamus!"* This should end the whole wretched business—this and the sack of the city. I hope Pollock won't be squeamish, or truckle to the hysterical party at home. The town should be laid in ashes and the fields sown with salt. Above all, the Residency and the Palace must come down. So shall Burnes, McNaghten, and many another gallant fellow know that his countrymen could avenge if they could not save him!

It is hard when others are gaining glory and experience to be stuck in this miserable valley. I have been out of it completely, bar a few petty skirmishes. However, we may see some service yet. A jemidar of ours brought in a hillman to-day, who says that the tribes are massing in the Terada ravine, ten miles to the north of us, and intend attacking the next convoy. We can't rely on information of this sort, but there may prove to be some truth in it. Proposed to shoot our informant, so as to prevent his playing the double traitor and reporting our proceedings. Elliott demurred. If you are making war you should throw no chance away. I hate half-and-half measures. The Children of Israel seem to have been the only people who ever carried war to its logical conclusion—except Cromwell in Ireland—made a compromise at last by which the man is to be detained as a prisoner and executed if his information prove to be false. I only hope we get a fair chance of showing what we can do. No doubt these fellows at the front will have C. B.'s and knighthoods showering upon them thick and fast, while we poor devils, who have had most of the responsibility and anxiety, will be passed over completely. Elliott has a whitlow. The last convoy left us a large packet of sauces, but as they forgot to leave anything to eat with them, we have handed them over to the Sowars, who drink them out of their pannikins as if they were liqueurs. We hear that another large convoy may be expected from the plains in the course of a day or two. Took nine to four on Cleopatra for the Calcutta Cup.

October 4.—The hillmen really mean business this time, I think. We have had two of our spies come in this morning with the same account about the gathering in the Terada quarter. That old rascal Zemaun is at the head of it, and I have recommended the Government to present him with a telescope in return for his neutrality! There will be no Zemaun to present it to if I can but lay hands upon him. We expect the convoy to-morrow morning, and need anticipate no attack until it comes up, for these fellows fight for plunder, not for glory, though, to do them justice, they have plenty of pluck when they get started. I have devised an excellent plan, and it has Elliott's hearty support. By Jove! if we can only manage it, it will be as pretty a ruse as ever I heard of! Our intention is to give out that we are going down the valley to meet the convoy and to block the mouth of a pass from which we profess to expect an attack. Very good. We shall make a night march to-night and reach their camp. Once there I shall conceal my two hundred men in the wagons and travel up with the convoy again. Our friends, the enemy, having heard that we intended to go south, and seeing the caravan going north without us, will naturally swoop down upon it under the impression that we are twenty miles away. We shall teach them such a lesson that they would as soon think of stopping a thunderbolt as of interfering again with one of Her Britannic Majesty's provision trains. I am all on thorns to be off.

Elliott has rigged up two of his guns so ingeniously that they look more like costermongers' barrows than anything else. To see artillery ready for action in the convoy might arouse suspicion. The artillerymen will be in the wagons next the guns, all ready to unlimber and open fire. Infantry in front and rear. Have told our confidential and discreet Sepoy servants the plan which we do *not* intend to adopt. N.B.—If you wish a thing to be noised over a whole province always whisper it under a vow of secrecy to your confidential native servant.

8:45 P.M.—Just starting for the convoy. May luck go with us!

October 5.—Seven o'clock in the evening. *Io triumphe!* Crown us with laurel—Elliott and myself! Who can compare with us as vermin-killers? I have only just got back, tired and weary, stained with blood and dust, but I have sat down before either washing or changing to have the satisfaction of seeing our deeds set forth in black and white—if only in my private log for no eye but my own. I shall describe it all fully as a preparation for our official account, which must be drawn up when Elliott gets back. Billy Dawson used to say that there were three degrees of comparison—a prevarication, a lie, and an official account. We at least cannot exaggerate our success, for it would be impossible to add anything to it.

We set out, then, as per programme, and came upon the camp near the head of the valley. They had two weak companies of the 54th with them who might no doubt have held their own with warning, but an unexpected rush of wild hillmen is a very difficult thing to stand against. With our reinforcement, however, and on our guard, we might defy the rascals. Chamberlain was in command—a fine young fellow. We soon made him understand the situation, and were all ready for a start by daybreak though his wagons were so full that we were compelled to leave several tons of fodder behind in order to make room for my Sepoys and for the artillery. About five o'clock we inspanned, to use an Africanism, and by six we were well on our way, with our escort as straggling and unconcerned as possible—as helpless-looking a caravan as ever invited attack.

I could soon see that it was to be no false alarm this time, and that the tribes really meant business. From my post of observation under the canvas screen of one of the wagons I could make our turbaned heads popping up to have a look at us from among the rocks, and an occasional scout hurrying northward with the news of our approach. It was not, however, until we came abreast of the Terada Pass, a gloomy defile bounded by gigantic cliffs, that the Afreedees began to show in force, though they had ambushed themselves so cleverly that had we not been keenly on the look-out for them, we might have walked right into the trap. As it was, the convoy halted, upon which the hillmen, seeing that they were observed, opened a heavy but ill-directed fire upon us. I had asked Chamberlain to throw out his men in skirmishing order, and to give them directions to retreat slowly upon the wagons so as to draw the Afreedees on. The ruse succeeded to perfection. As the redcoats steadily re-tired, keeping behind cover as much as possible, the enemy followed them up with yells of exultation, springing from rock to rock, waving their jezails in the air, and howling like a pack of demons. With their black, contorted, mocking faces, their fierce gestures, and their fluttering garments, they would have made a study for any painter who wished to portray Milton's conception of the army of the damned. From every side they pressed in until seeing, as they thought, nothing between them and victory. They left the shelter of the rocks and came rushing down, a furi-ous, howling throng, with the green banner of the Prophet in their van. Now was our chance, and gloriously we utilized it. From every cranny and slit of the wagons came a blaze of fire, every shot of which told among the close-packed mob. Two or three score rolled over like rabbits and the rest reeled for a mo-ment, and then, with their chiefs at their heads, came on again in a magnificent rush. It was useless, however, for undisciplined men to attempt to face such a well-directed fire. The leaders were bowled over, and the others, after hesitating for a few mo-ments, turned and made for the rocks. It was our turn now to assume the offensive. The guns were unlimbered and grape poured into them, while our little infantry force advanced at the double, shooting and stabbing all whom they overtook. Never have I known the tide of battle turn so rapidly and so decisively. The sullen retreat became a flight, and the flight a panic-stricken rout, until there was nothing left of the tribesmen except a scat-tered, demoralized rabble flying wildly to their native fastnesses for shelter and protection.

I was by no means inclined to let them off cheaply now that I had them in my power. On the contrary, I determined to teach them such a lesson that the sight of a single scarlet uniform would in future be a passport in itself. We followed hard upon the track of the fugitives and entered the Terada defile at their very heels. Having detached Chamberlain and Elliott with a company on either side to protect my wings, I pushed on with

my Sepoys and a handful of artillerymen, giving them no time to
rally or to recover themselves. We were so handicapped, however, by our stiff European uniforms and by our want of practise
in climbing, that we should have been unable to overtake any of
the mountaineers had it not been for a fortunate accident.
There is a smaller ravine which opens into the main pass, and in
their hurry and confusion some of the fugitives rushed down
this. I saw sixty or seventy of them turn down, but I should have
passed them by and continued in pursuit of the main body had
not one of my scouts come rushing up to inform me that the
smaller ravine was a *cul-de-sac*, and that the Afreedees who had
gone up it had no possible means of getting out again except by
cutting their way through our ranks. Here was an opportunity of
striking terror into the tribes. Leaving Chamberlain and Elliott
to continue the pursuit of the main body, I wheeled my Sepoys
into the narrow pass and proceeded slowly down it in extended
order, covering the whole ground from cliff to cliff. Not a jackal
could have passed unseen. The rebels were caught like rats in a
trap.

The defile in which we found ourselves was the most gloomy
and majestic that I have ever seen. On either side naked preci-
pices rose sheer up for a thousand feet or more, converging
upon each other so as to leave a very narrow slit of daylight
above us, which was further reduced by the feathery fringe of
palm trees and aloes which hung over each lip of the chasm. The
cliffs were not more than a couple of hundred yards apart at the
entrance, but as we advanced they grew nearer and nearer, until
a half company in close order could hardly march abreast. A sort
of twilight reigned in this strange valley, and the dim, uncertain
light made the great basalt rocks loom up vague and fantastic.
There was no path, and the ground was most uneven, but I
pushed on briskly, cautioning my fellows to have their fingers on
their triggers, for I could see that we were nearing the point
where the two cliffs would form an acute angle with each
other.

At last we came in sight of the place. A great pile of boulders
were heaped up at the very end of the pass, and among these
our fugitives were skulking, entirely demoralized apparently,

and incapable of resistance. They were useless as prisoners, and it was out of the question to let them go, so there was no choice but to polish them off. Waving my sword, I was leading my men on, when we had a most dramatic interruption of a sort which I have seen once or twice on the boards of Drury Lane, but never in real life.

In the side of the cliff, close to the pile of stones where the hillmen were making their last stand, there was a cave which looked more like the lair of some wild beast than a human habitation. Out of this dark archway there suddenly emerged an old man—such a very, very old man that all the other veterans whom I have seen were as chickens compared to him. His hair and his beard were both as white as snow, and each reached more than half way to his waist. His face was wrinkled and brown and bony, a cross between a monkey and a mummy, and so thin and emaciated were his shrivelled limbs that you would hardly have given him credit for having any vitality left, were it not for his eyes, which glittered and sparkled with excitement, like two diamonds in a setting of mahogany. This apparition came rushing out of the cave, and, throwing himself between the fugitives and our fellows, motioned us back with as imperious a sweep of the hand as ever an emperor used to his slaves.

"Men of blood," he cried, in a voice of thunder, speaking excellent English, too—"this is a place for prayer and meditation, not for murder. Desist, lest the wrath of the gods fall upon you!"

"Stand aside, old man," I shouted. "You will meet with a hurt if you don't get out of the way."

I could see that the hillmen were taking heart, and that some of my Sepoys were flinching, as if they did not relish this new enemy. Clearly, I must act promptly, if I wished to complete our success. I dashed forward at the head of the white artillerymen who had stuck to me. The old fellow rushed at us with his arms out as if to stop us; but it was no time to stick at trifles, so I passed my sword through his body at the same moment that one of the gunners brought his carbine down upon his head. He dropped instantly, and the hillmen, at the sight of his fall, set up the most unearthly howl of horror and consternation. The Sepoys, who had been inclined to hang back, came on again the moment he was disposed of, and it did not take us long to consummate our victory. Hardly a man of the enemy got out of the defile alive. What could Hannibal or Cæsar have done more? Our own loss in the whole affair has been insignificant—three killed and about fifteen wounded. Got their banner, a green wisp of a thing with a sentence of the Koran engraved upon it.

I looked, after the action, for the old chap, but his body had disappeared, though how or whither I have no conception. His blood be upon his own head! He would be alive now if he had not interfered, as the constables say at home, "with an officer in the execution of his duty." The scouts tell me that his name was Ghoolab Shah, and that he was one of the highest and holiest of the Buddhists. He had great fame in the district as a prophet and worker of miracles—hence the hubbub when he was cut down. They tell me that he was living in this very cave when Tamerlane passed this way in 1397, with a lot more bosh of the sort. I went into the cave, and how any man could live in it a week is a mystery to me, for it was little more than four feet high, and as damp and dismal a grotto as ever was seen. A wooden settle and a rough table was the sole furniture, with a lot of parchment scrolls covered with hieroglyphics. Well, he has gone where he will learn that the gospel of peace and goodwill is superior to all his Pagan lore. Peace go with him!

Elliott and Chamberlain never caught the main body—I knew they wouldn't—so the honors of the day rest with me. I ought to get a step for it, anyhow, and perhaps, who knows? some mention in the *Gazette*. What a lucky chance! I think Zemaun deserves his telescope after all for giving it to me. Shall have something to eat now, for I am half starved. Glory is an excellent thing, but you cannot live upon it.

October 6, 11 A.M.—Let me try to set down as calmly and as accurately as I can all that occurred last night. I have never been a dreamer or a visionary, so I can rely upon my own senses, though I am bound to say that if any other fellow had told me the same thing I should have doubted him. I might even have suspected that I was deceived at the time had I not heard the bell since. However, I must narrate what happened.

Elliott was in my tent with me having a quiet cheroot until about ten o'clock. I then walked the rounds with my jemidar, and having seen that all was right I turned in a little before eleven. I was just dropping off to sleep, for I was dog-tired after the day's work, when I was aroused by some slight noise, and, looking round, I saw a man dressed in Asiatic costume standing at the entrance of my tent. He was motionless when I saw him, and he had his eyes fixed upon me with a solemn and stern expression. My first thought was that the fellow was some Ghazi or Afghan fanatic who had stolen in with the intention of stabbing me, and with this idea in my mind I had all the will to spring from my couch and defend myself, but the power was unaccountably lacking. An overpowering languor and want of energy possessed me. Had I seen the dagger descending upon my breast I could not have made an effort to avert it. I suppose a bird when it is under the influence of a snake feels very much as I did in the presence of this gloomy-faced stranger. My mind was clear enough, but my body was as torpid as though I were still asleep. I shut my eyes once or twice and tried to persuade myself that the whole thing was a delusion, but every time that I opened them there was the man still regarding me with the same stony, menacing stare. The silence became unendurable. I felt that I must overcome my languor so far as to address him. I am not a nervous man, and I never knew before what Virgil meant when he wrote "*adhœsit faucibus ora.*" At last I managed to stammer out a few words, asking the intruder who he was and what he wanted.

"Lieutenant Heatherstone," he answered, speaking slowly and gravely, "you have committed this day the foulest sacrilege and the greatest crime which it is possible for man to do. You have slain one of the thrice blessed and reverent ones, an arch adept of the first degree, an elder brother who has trod the higher path for more years than you have numbered months. You have cut him off at a time when his labors promised to reach a climax, and when he was about to attain a height of occult knowledge which would have brought man one step nearer to the Creator. All this you have done without excuse, with provocation, at a time when he was pleading the cause of the helpless and distressed. Listen now to me, John Heatherstone.

"When first the occult sciences were pursued many thousands of years ago, it was found by the learned that the short tenure of human existence was too limited to allow a man to attain the loftiest heights of inner life. The inquirers of those days directed their energies in the first place, therefore, to the lengthening of their own days in order that they might have more scope for improvement. By their knowledge of the secret laws of Nature they were enabled to fortify their bodies against disease and old age. It only remained to protect themselves against the assaults of wicked and violent men who are ever ready to destroy what is wiser and nobler than themselves. There was no direct means by which this protection could be effected, but it was in some measures attained by arranging the occult forces in such a way that a terrible and unavoidable retribution should await the offender. It was irrevocably ordained by laws which cannot be reversed that any one who should shed the blood of a brother who had attained a certain degree of sanctity should be a doomed man. Those laws are extant to this day, John Heatherstone, and you have placed yourself in their power. King or emperor would be helpless before the forces which you have called into play. What hope, then, is there for you?

"In former days these laws acted so instantaneously that the slayer perished with his victim. It was judged afterwards that this prompt retribution prevented the offender from having time to realize the enormity of his offense. It was therefore ordained that in all such cases the retribution should be left in the hands of the chelas, or immediate disciples of the holy man, with power to extend or shorten it at their will, exacting it either at the time or at any future anniversary of the day when the crime was committed. Why punishment should come on those days only it does not concern you to know. Suffice it that you are the murderer of Ghoolab Shah, the thrice blessed, and that I am the senior of his three chelas commissioned to avenge his death.

"It is no personal matter between us. Amid our studies we have no leisure or inclination for personal matters. It is an immutable law, and it is as impossible for us to relax it as it is for you to escape from it. Sooner or later we shall come to you and claim your life in atonement for the one which you have taken. The same fate shall be meted out to the wretched soldier, Smith, who, though less guilty than yourself, has incurred the same penalty by raising his sacrilegious hand against the chosen of Buddha. If your life is prolonged it is merely that you may have time to repent of your misdeed and to feel the full force of your punishment. And lest you should be tempted to cast it out of your mind and to forget it, our bell—our astral bell, the use of which is one of our occult secrets—shall ever remind you of what has been and what is to be. You shall hear it by day and you shall hear it by night, and it will be a sign to you that, do what you may and go where you will, you can never shake yourself clear of the chelas of Ghoolab Shah. You will never see me more, accursed one, until the day when we come for you. Live in fear, and in that anticipation which is worse than death." With a menacing wave of the hand the figure turned and swept out of my tent into the darkness.

The instant that the fellow disappeared from my sight I recovered from the lethargy which had fallen upon me. Springing to my feet, I rushed to the opening and looked out. A Sepoy sentry was standing leaning upon his musket, a few paces off.

"You dog," I said in Hindustani. "What do you mean by letting people disturb me in this way?"

The man stared at me in amazement. "Has any one disturbed the Sahib?" he asked.

"This instant—this moment. You must have seen him pass out of my tent."

"Surely the Burra Sahib is mistaken," the man answered, respectfully but firmly. "I have been here for an hour, and no one has passed from the tent."

Puzzled and disconcerted, I was sitting by the side of my couch wondering whether the whole thing was a delusion, brought on by the nervous excitement of our skirmish, when a new marvel overtook me. From over my head there suddenly sounded a sharp, tinkling sound, like that produced by an empty glass when flipped by the nail, only louder and more intense. I looked up, but nothing was to be seen. I examined the whole interior of the tent carefully, but without discovering any cause for the strange sound. At last, worn out with fatigue, I gave the mystery up, and throwing myself upon the couch was soon fast asleep. When I woke this morning I was inclined to put the whole of my yesterday night's experiences down to imagination, but I was soon disabused of the idea, for I had hardly risen before the same strange sound was repeated in my very ear as loudly, and to all appearance as causelessly, as before. What it is or where it comes from I cannot conceive. I have not heard it since. Can the fellow's threats have something in them and this be the warning bell of which he spoke? Surely it is impossible. Yet his manner was indescribably impressive. I have tried to set down what he said as accurately as I can, but I fear I have omitted a good deal. What is to be the end of this strange affair? I must go in for a course of religion and holy water. Not a word to Chamberlain or Elliott. They tell me I am looking like a ghost this morning.

Evening.—Have managed to compare notes with Gunner Rufus Smith of the Artillery, who knocked the old fellow over with the butt of his gun. His experience has been the same as mine. He has heard the sound too. What is the meaning of it all? My brain is in a whirl.

Oct. 10 (four days later).—God help us!

This last laconic entry terminated the journal. It seemed to me that coming as it did after four days' complete silence it told a clearer tale of a shaken nerve and a broken spirit than could any more elaborate narrative. Pinned on to the journal was a supplementary statement which had evidently been recently added by the general.

"From that day to this," it said, "I have had no night or day free from the intrusion of that dreadful sound with its accompanying train of thought. Time and custom have brought me no relief, but, on the contrary, as the years pass over my head my physical strength decreases and my nerves become less able to bear up against the continual strain. I am a broken man in mind and body. I live in a state of tension, always straining my ears for the hated sound, afraid to converse with my fellows for fear of exposing my dreadful condition to them, with no comfort or hope of comfort on this side of the grave. I should be willing, Heaven knows, to die, and yet as each 5th of October comes round, I am prostrated with fear because I do not know what strange and terrible experience may be in store for me. Forty years have passed since I slew Ghoolab Shah, and forty times I have gone through all the horrors of death, without attaining the blessed peace which lies beyond. I have no means of knowing in what shape my fate will come upon me. I have immured myself in this lonely country, and surrounded myself with barriers, because in my weaker moments my instincts urge me to take some steps for self-protection, but I know well in my heart how futile it all is. They must come quickly now for I grow old, and Nature will forestall them unless they make haste.

"I take credit to myself that I have kept my hands off the prussic acid or opium bottle. It has always been in my power to checkmate my occult persecutors in that way, but I have ever held that a man in this world cannot desert his post until he has been relieved in due course by the authorities. I have had no scruples, however, about exposing myself to danger, and during the Sikh and Sepoy wars I did all that a man could do to court death. He passed me by, however, and picked out many a young fellow to whom life was only opening and who had everything to live for, while I survived to win crosses and honors which had lost all relish for me. Well, well, these things cannot depend upon chance, and there is no doubt some deep reason for it all. One compensation Providence has made me in the shape of a true and faithful wife, to whom I told my dreadful secret before the wedding, and who nobly consented to share my lot. She has lifted half the burden from my shoulders, but with the effect, poor soul, of crushing her own life beneath its weight. My children, too, have been a comfort to me. Mordaunt knows all, or nearly all. Gabriel we have endeavored to keep in the dark, though we can not prevent her from knowing that there is something amiss. I should like this statement to be shown to Dr. John Easterling, of Stranraer. He heard on one occasion this haunting sound. My sad experience may show him that I spoke truth when I said that there was much knowledge in the world which has never found its way to England yet.

"J. B. HEATHERSTONE."

It was going on for dawn by the time that I had finished this extraordinary narrative, to which my sister and Mordaunt Heatherstone listened with the most absorbed attention. Already we could see through the window that the stars had begun to fade and a grey light to appear in the east. The crofter who owned the lurcher dog lived a couple of miles off, so it was time for us to be on foot. Leaving Esther to tell my father the story in such fashion as she might, we thrust some food in our pockets and set off upon our solemn and eventful errand.

CHAPTER XVI

AT THE HOLE OF CREE

IT was dark enough when we started to make it no easy matter to find our way across the moors, but as we advanced it grew lighter and lighter, until by the time we reached Fullarton's cabin it was broad daylight. Early as it was, he was up and about, for the Wigtown peasants are an early rising race. We explained our mission to him in as few words as possible, and having made his bargain—what Scot ever neglected that preliminary—he agreed not only to let us have the use of his dog but to come with us himself. Mordaunt, in his desire for privacy, would have demurred at this arrangement, but I pointed out to him that we had no idea what was in store for us, and the addition of a strong, able-bodied man to our party might prove to be of the utmost consequence. Again, the dog was less likely to give us trouble if we had its master to control it. My arguments carried the day, and the biped accompanied us as well as his four-footed companion.

There was some little similarity between the two, for the man was a tousy-headed fellow with a great mop of yellow hair and a straggling beard, while the dog was of the long-haired, unkempt breed looking like an animated bundle of oakum. All our way to the Hall its owner kept retailing instances of the creature's sagacity and powers of scent, which, according to his account, were little less than miraculous. His anecdotes had a poor audience, I fear, for my mind was filled with the strange story which I had been reading, while Mordaunt strolled on with wild eyes and feverish cheeks, without a thought for anything but the problem which we had to solve. Again and again as we topped

131

an eminence, I saw him look eagerly round him in the faint hope of seeing some trace of the absentee, but over the whole expanse of moorland there was no sign of movement or of life. All was dead and silent and deserted.

Our visit to the Hall was a very brief one, for every minute now was of importance. Mordaunt rushed in and emerged with an old coat of his father's, which he handed to Fullarton, who held it out to the dog. The intelligent brute sniffed at it all over, then ran whining a little way down the avenue, came back to sniff the coat again, and finally elevating its stump of a tail in triumph, uttered a succession of sharp yelps to show that it was satisfied that it had struck the trail. Its owner tied a long cord to its collar to prevent it from going too fast for us, and we all set off upon our search, the dog tugging and straining at its leash in its excitement as it followed in the general's footsteps.

Our way lay for a couple of hundred yards along the high road, and then passed through a gap in the hedge and on to the moor, across which we were led in a bee-line to the northward. The sun had by this time risen above the horizon, and the whole countryside looked so fresh and sweet, from the blue, sparkling sea to the purple mountains, that it was difficult to realize how weird and uncanny was the enterprise upon which we were engaged.

The scent must have lain strongly upon the ground, for the dog never hesitated nor stopped, dragging its master along at a pace which rendered conversation impossible. At one place, in crossing a small stream, we seemed to get off the trail for a few minutes, but our keen-nosed ally soon picked it up upon the other side and followed it over the trackless moor, whining and yelping all the time in its eagerness. Had we not all three been fleet of foot and long of wind, we could not have persisted in the continuous rapid journey over the roughest of ground, with the heather often well-nigh up to our waists.

For my own part, I have no idea now, looking back, what goal it was which I expected to reach at the end of our pursuit. I can remember that my mind was full of the vaguest and most varying speculations. Could it be that the three Buddhists had had a craft in readiness off the coast, and had embarked with their prisoners for the East? The direction of their track seemed at first to favor this supposition, for it lay in the line of the upper end of the bay, but it ended by branching off and striking inland. Clearly the ocean was not to be our terminus.

By ten o'clock we had walked close upon twelve miles, and were compelled to call a halt for a few minutes to recover our breath, for the last mile or two we had been breasting the long, wearying slope of the Wigtown hills. From the summit of this range, which is nowhere more than a thousand feet in height, we could see, looking northward, such a scene of bleakness and desolation as can hardly be matched in any country. Right away to the horizon stretched the broad expanse of mud and of water, mingled and mixed together in the wildest chaos, like a portion of some world in the process of formation. Here and there on the dun-colored surface of this great marsh there had burst out patches of sickly yellow reeds and of livid, greenish scum, which only served to heighten and intensify the gloomy effect of the dull, melancholy expanse. On the side nearest to us some abandoned peat cuttings showed that ubiquitous man had been at work there, but beyond these few petty scars there was no sign anywhere of human life. Not even a crow or a seagull flapped their way over that hideous desert.

This is the great bog of Cree, which may be seen in the maps to extend over a considerable surface of the shire of Wigtown. It is a salt-water marsh formed by an inroad of the sea, and so intersected is it with dangerous swamps and treacherous pitfalls of liquid mud, that no man would venture through it unless he had the guidance of one of the few peasants who retain the secret of its paths. As we approached the fringe of rushes which marked its border, a foul, dank smell rose up from the stagnant wilderness, as from impure water and decaying vegetation—an earthy, noisome smell which poisoned the fresh, upland air. So forbidding and gloomy was the aspect of the place that our stout crofter hesitated, and it was all that we could do to persuade him to proceed. Our lurcher, however, not being subject to the delicate impressions of our higher organizations, still ran yelping along with its nose on the ground and every fibre of its body quivering with excitement and eagerness.

There was no difficulty about picking our way through the morass, for wherever the five could go we three could follow. If we could have had any doubts as to our dog's guidance they would all have been removed now, for in the soft, black, oozing soil we could distinctly trace the tracks of the whole party. From these we could see that they had walked abreast, and, furthermore, that each was about equi-distant from the other. Clearly, then, no physical force had been used in taking the general and his companion along. The compulsion had been psychical and not material.

Once within the swamp we had to be careful not to deviate from the narrow track, which offered a firm foothold. On each side lay shallow sheets of stagnant water overlying a treacherous bottom of semifluid mud, which rose above the surface here and there in moist, sweltering banks, mottled over with occasional patches of unhealthy vegetation. Great purple and yellow fungi had broken out in a dense eruption, as though nature were afflicted with a foul disease, which manifested itself by this crop of plague spots. Here and there dark, crab-like creatures scuttled across our path, and hideous, flesh-colored worms wriggled and writhed amid the sickly reeds. Swarms of buzzing, piping insects rose up at every step and formed a dense cloud around our heads, settling on our hands and faces and inoculating us with their filthy venom. Never had I ventured into so pestilent and forbidding a place. Mordaunt Heatherstone strode on, however, with a set purpose upon his swarthy brow, and we could but follow him, determined to stand by him to the end of the adventure.

As we advanced the path grew narrower and narrower until, as we saw by the tracks, our predecessors had been compelled to walk in single file. Fullarton was leading us with the dog, Mordaunt behind him, while I brought up the rear. The peasant had been sulky and surly for a little time back, hardly answering when spoken to, but he now stopped short and positively refused to go a step further.

"It's no canny," he said; "besides, I ken where it will lead us tae!"

"Where, then?" I asked.

"Tae the Hole o' Cree," he answered. "It's no far frae here I'm thinking."

"The Hole of Cree! What is that, then?"

"It's a great, muckle hole in the ground that gangs awa' doun so deep that naebody could ever reach the bottom. Indeed there are folk wha say that it's just a door leadin' intae the bottomless pit itsel'."

"You have been there, then?" I asked.

"Been there!" he cried. "What would I be doin' at the Hole o' Cree? No, I've never been there, nor any other man in his senses."

"How do you know about it, then?"

"My great grandfeyther had been there, and that's how I ken," Fullarton answered. "He was fou' one Saturday nicht and he went for a bet. He didna like tae talk aboot it afterwards, and he wouldna' tell a' what befell him, but he was aye feared o' the very name. He's the first Fullarton that's been at the Hole o' Cree, and he'll be the last for me. If ye'll tak' my advice ye'll just gie the matter up and gang hame again for there's no guid tae be got oot o' this place."

"We shall go on with you or without you," Mordaunt answered. "Let us have your dog and we can pick you up on our way back."

"Na, na," he cried; "I'll no hae my dog scared wi' bogles and running down Auld Nick as if he were a hare. The dog shall bide wi' me."

"The dog shall go with us," said my companion, with his eyes blazing. "We have no time to argue with you. Here's a five-pound note. Let us have the dog, or, by heavens, I shall take it by force and throw you in the bog if you hinder us." I could realize the Heatherstone of forty years ago when I saw the fierce and sudden wrath which lit up the features of his son.

Either the bribe or the threat had the desired effect; for the fellow grabbed at the money with one hand while with the other he surrendered the leash which held the lurcher. Leaving him to retrace his steps, we continued to make our way into the utmost recesses of the great swamp. The tortuous path grew less and less defined as we proceeded, and was even covered in

places with water; but the increasing excitement of the hound
and the sight of the deep foot-marks in the mud, stimulated us
to push on. At last, after struggling through a grove of high bul-
rushes, we came on a spot the gloomy horror of which might
have furnished Danté with a fresh terror for his Inferno.

The whole bog in this part appeared to have sunk in, forming
a great funnel-shaped depression, which terminated in the centre in a circular rift or opening about forty paces in diameter. It
was a whirlpool—a perfect maelstrom of mud sloping down on
every side to this silent and awful chasm. Clearly this was the
spot which, under the name of the Hole of Cree, bore such a
sinister reputation among the rustics. I could not wonder at its
impressing their imagination, for a weirder or more gloomy
scene, or one more worthy of the avenue which led to it, could
not be conceived. The steps passed down the declivity which
surrounded the abyss, and we followed them with a sinking feeling in our hearts, as we realized that this was the end of our
search. A little way from the downward path was the return trail
made by the feet of those who had come back from the chasm's
edge. Our eyes fell upon these tracks at the same moment, and
we each gave a cry of horror, and stood gazing speechlessly at
them. For there, in those blurred footmarks, the whole drama
was revealed. *Five had gone down, but only three had
returned.*

None shall ever know the details of that strange tragedy.
There was no mark of struggle or sign of attempt at escape. We
knelt at the edge of the Hole and endeavored to pierce the un-
fathomable gloom which surrounded it. A faint, sickly exhalation
seemed to rise from its depths, and there was a distant, hurrying, clattering sound as of waters in the bowels of the earth. A
great stone lay embedded in the mud, and this I hurled over, but
we never heard thud or splash to show that it had reached the
bottom. As we hung over the noisome chasm a sound did at last
rise to our ears out of its murky depths. High, clear, and throbbing, it tinkled for an instant out of the abyss, to be succeeded
by the same deadly stillness which had preceded it. I do not
wish to appear to be superstitious, or to put down to extraordinary causes that which may have a natural explanation. That one

keen note may have been some strange water sound produced far down in the bowels of the earth. It may have been that or it may have been that sinister bell of which I had heard so much. Be this as it may, it was the only sign that rose to us from the last terrible resting-place of the two who had paid the debt which had so long been owing.

We joined our voices in a call with the unreasoning obstinacy with which men will cling to hope, but no answer came back to us save a thousand hollow reverberations from the depths beneath. Footsore and heart-sick, we retraced our steps and climbed the slimy slope once more.

"What shall we do, Mordaunt?" I asked, in a subdued voice. "We can but pray that their souls may rest in peace."

Young Heatherstone looked at me with flashing eyes. "This may be all according to occult laws," he cried, "but we shall see what the laws of England have to say upon it. I suppose a chela may be hanged as well as any other man. It may not be too late yet to run them down. Here, good dog, good dog—here!" He pulled the hound over and set it on the track of the three men. The creature sniffed at it once or twice, and then, falling upon its stomach, with bristling hair and protruding tongue, it lay shivering and trembling, a very embodiment of canine terror.

"You see," I said, "it is no use contending against those who have powers at their command which we cannot even give a name to. There is nothing for it but to accept the inevitable, and to hope that these poor men may meet with some compensation in another world for all that they have suffered in this."

"And be free from all devilish religions and their murderous worshippers!" Mordaunt cried, furiously.

Justice compelled me to acknowledge in my own heart that the murderous spirit had been set on foot by the Christian before it was taken up by the Buddhists, but I forebore to remark upon it for fear of irritating my companion. For a long time I could not draw him away from the scene of his father's death, but at last, by repeated arguments and reasonings, I succeeded in making him realize how useless and unprofitable any further efforts on our part must necessarily prove, and in inducing him to return with me to Cloomber. Oh! the wearisome, tedious journey! It had seemed long enough when we had some slight flicker of hope, or at least of expectation, before us, but now that our worst fears were fulfilled it appeared interminable. We picked up our peasant guide at the outskirts of the marsh, and having restored his dog we let him find his own way home, without telling him anything of the results of our expedition. We ourselves plodded all day over the moors with heavy feet and heavier hearts until we saw the ill-omened tower of Cloomber, and at last, as the sun was setting, found ourselves once more beneath its roof.

There is no need for me to enter into further details, or to describe the grief which our tidings conveyed to mother and to daughter. Their long expectation of some calamity was not sufficient to prepare them for the terrible reality. For weeks my poor Gabriel hovered between life and death, and though she came round at last, thanks to the nursing of my sister and the professional skill of Dr. John Easterling, of Stranraer, she has never to this day entirely recovered her former vigor. Mordaunt, too, suffered much for some time, and it was only after our removal to Edinburgh that he rallied from the shock which he had undergone. As to poor Mrs. Heatherstone, neither medical attention nor change of air can ever have a permanent effect upon her. Slowly and surely, but very placidly, she has declined in health and strength, until it is evident that in a very few weeks at the most she will have rejoined her husband and restored to him the one thing which he must have grudged to leave behind.

The Laird of Branksome came home from Italy restored in health, with the result that we were compelled to return once more to Edinburgh. The change was agreeable to us, for recent events had cast a cloud over our country life and had surrounded us with unpleasant associations. Besides, a highly honorable and remunerative appointment in connection with the University library had become vacant, and had, through the kindness of the late Sir Alexander Grant, been offered to my father, who, as may be imagined, lost no time in accepting so congenial a post. In this way we came back to Edinburgh very much more important people than we left it, and with no further reason to be uneasy about the details of housekeeping. But, in truth, the whole household has been dissolved, for I have been married for some months to my dear Gabriel, and Esther is to become Mrs. Heatherstone upon the 23rd of the month. If she makes him as good a wife as his sister has made to me, we may both set ourselves down as fortunate men.

These mere domestic episodes are, as I have already explained, introduced only because I cannot avoid alluding to them. My object in drawing up this statement and publishing the evidence which corroborates it, was certainly not to parade my private affairs before the public, but to leave on record an authentic narrative of a most remarkable series of events. This I have endeavored to do in as methodical a manner as possible, exaggerating nothing and suppressing nothing. The reader has now the evidence before him, and can form his own opinions unaided by me as to the causes of the disappearance and death of Rufus Smith and of John Berthier Heatherstone, V.C., C.B.

There is only one point which is still dark to me. Why the chelas of Ghoolab Shah should have removed their victims to the desolate Hole of Cree instead of taking their lives at Cloomber, is, I confess, a mystery to me. In dealing with occult laws, however, we must allow for our own complete ignorance of the subject. Did we know more we might see that there was some analogy between that foul bog and the sacrilege which had been committed, and that their ritual and customs demanded that just such a death was the one appropriate to the crime. On this point I should be sorry to be dogmatic, but at least we must allow that the Buddhist priests must have had some very good cause for the course of action which they so deliberately carried out.

Months afterwards I saw a short paragraph in the *Star of India* announcing that three eminent Buddhists—Lal Hoomi, Mowdar Khan and Ram Singh—had just returned in the steamship *Deccan* from a short trip to Europe. The very next item was devoted to an account of the life and services of Major-General Heatherstone, "who has lately disappeared from his country house in Wigtownshire, and who, there is too much reason to fear, has been drowned." I wonder if by chance there was any other human eye but mine which traced a connection between these paragraphs. I never showed them to my wife or to Mordaunt, and they will only know of their existence when they read these pages.

I don't know that there is any other point which needs clearing up. The intelligent reader will have already seen the reasons for the general's fear of dark faces, of wandering men (not knowing how his pursuers might come after him), of visitors (from the same cause and because his hateful bell was liable to sound at all times). His broken sleep led him to wander about the house at night, and the lamps which he burned in every room were no doubt to prevent his imagination from peopling the darkness with terrors. Lastly, his elaborate precautions were as he has himself explained, rather the result of a feverish desire to do something than in the expectation that he could really ward off his fate.

Science will tell you that there are no such powers as those claimed by the Eastern mystics. I, John Fothergill West, can confidently answer that science is wrong, and invite the reader's attention to a pithy, if disrespectful, aphorism of Baron Hellenbach. For what is science? Science is the consensus of opinion of scientific men, and history has shown that it is slow to accept a truth. Science sneered at Newton for twenty years. Science proved mathematically that an iron ship could not swim, and science declared that a steamship could not cross the Atlantic. Like Goethe's Mephistopheles, our wise professor's forte is to *"stets verneinen."* Thomas Didymus is, to use his own jargon, his prototype. Let him learn that if he will but cease to believe in the infallibility of his own methods, and will look to the East, from which all great movements come, he will find there a school of philosophers and of savants who, working on different lines to his own, are many thousand years ahead of him in all the essentials of knowledge.

THE OCCULT PHILOSOPHY

ADDENDUM

BY MR. MORDAUNT HEATHERSTONE

I HAVE just looked over the proof sheets of my good friend's account of the events which led up to the death of my father, and I am able to endorse it on every point—save, indeed that he lays too little stress on the kindness and devotion which he displayed himself throughout. I have asked him, however, before sending his proofs finally to the press, to allow me to make this small addition in order that I may say a few words upon these Indian occults of whom so little is known. In this appendix form, any reader is at liberty to neglect it; but should he be interested in the subject, I have endeavored to collect a little information for him.

The Eastern adepts exist at present principally in the north of India and in Thibet, though in former days it is probable that their organization was much more widespread. Under the various names of the Egyptian priests, Chaldean Magi, Essenes, Gnostics, Theurgic Neo-Platonists, and Seers, we catch glimpses of them throughout history. They form the closest and most important secret society which has ever been organized—a society to which any suitable man may gain admission, but which is girt round with such physical terrors, so much bodily privation and discipline, that few have the courage and hardihood to persevere to the end. Those who are earnest and resolute enough to attain full initiation have, however, their full reward for all that they have gone through, for they attain such knowledge and such powers as raise them far above the ruck of mankind.

141

The knowledge of the occult philosophers is both physical and metaphysical, but it is to the latter branch, and especially to the human soul and its destiny, that they have devoted most attention. Their physical knowledge, however, and their power of manipulating those secret laws by which Nature builds or destroys, are far in excess of anything known to European science. It must be remembered that our own scientific results are the results of a few hundred years, whereas the occult philosophy has been the work of the very cream of humanity, extending over an unbroken period of at least twenty thousand years, during which time every adept has handed down his powers to his initiates exactly as they were handed down to him, or with such additions as his life of study has enabled him to make. Wonderful as are the powers to which these men have attained, they are the first to disclaim any supernatural source for them. They arise entirely from an intimate knowledge of the nature of things and a deep insight into the hidden forces which pervade the universe. The whole race may hope some day to attain the learning which they have already acquired.

One of the first lessons which the occult initiate has to learn is that wisdom is not to be implanted in any mind by the mere process of study and of instruction. The soil must be prepared before this most precious seed can be committed to it. The keenest and most receptive intellect which is the seat also of pride, of avarice, of sensuality, of selfishness or the love of comfort, can never hope to surmount the first of the ordeals which the occult aspirant has to pass. These weeds must all be thoroughly and remorselessly eradicated before the garden can be planted. For seven years the young chela devotes himself to this struggle for the mastery over himself, until, if he be successful, he finds himself pure in mind and body, free from gross animal instincts, indifferent to personal comfort, and with all the spiritual part of his nature developed at the expense of the bestial. He is then in a condition to receive the first teachings which will lead him on to the higher path. Many, of course, break down in this preliminary process, and are never deemed worthy of the honor of initiation; but the very essence of the order is that it should be select. In this way the early training comes from within, not from without. To use their own expression, "an adept becomes—he is not made."

And what are the results obtained by this most ancient and stringent school of knowledge? By the very nature of things we outsiders can only have vague ideas of the few which are adapted to our understanding. The little which we know is probably the mere fringe of the subject. Yet they comprise some fairly weighty adjuncts to our stock of facts.

In the first place, they have proved without the shadow of a doubt that man possesses a soul by the simple expedient of separating it from the body and of rejoining them at pleasure. An adept can put off his body as he would put off his greatcoat, and can travel in his soul with the rapidity of thought to the other end of the world. This endows him with practical omniscience as far as mundane affairs are concerned. Again, they have satisfied themselves that the soul is itself a material thing, containing within it a far more ethereal essence, known as the spirit. When Paul of Tarsus says that man consists of a body, a soul and a spirit, he is not indulging in vain surmise, but is stating concisely the conclusions arrived at by the occult school to which there is every reason to think that he belonged.

Again, the adepts claim to communicate with each other by means of thought-transferrence and not by words. The initiated can therefore talk as easily at the distance of a thousand miles as if they were in the same room. Their desolate retreats and caves in the Himalayas, which seem so lonely to the ignorant, are really foci of mental activity and interchange of views. To attract each other's attention when they wish to communicate, they have the power of sounding that bell-like, tingling alarm which played so prominent a part in the case of my poor father.

They assert again, and support their assertion by proofs, that they have such a mastery over the subtle chemistry of Nature that they can take the elements from the atmosphere and combine them or mould them into any form they please, so as to make any visible object by the synthesis of invisible atoms. They can resolve a solid substance into its most minute molecules, waft those molecules on an occult current to any distance, and there untie them so as to form the original object exactly as it was before. In this manner a block of marble has been conveyed in an instant from Bombay to Calcutta, and letters have been sent with a rapidity which would render the telegraph obsolete.

These are one or two of their minor results claimed by the Eastern philosophers, and surely, if they profess to have attained nothing else, their system deserves some attention from the scientists of the West. The adepts themselves, however, in discussing the question, dismiss these physical phenomena as puerile manifestations, useful enough for service in this world, but of no permanent or real importance. The real value of their system lies, they declare, in its metaphysical or religious aspect, and there they claim to have cast a flood of light upon the destiny of the soul which will change religion from a mere speculation or aspiration to one of the exact science as demonstrable and as certain as geometry. Into these higher regions of the esoteric system none can penetrate save those who have already mastered the inferior grades, and been chastened in mind and body.

Of course the objection would at once occur to any Western reader that it was extremely improbable that a clique of men could keep their knowledge to themselves, and that if it were possible it is still reprehensible, since such knowledge is intended for the use of the whole human race. To this the occultist replies that the powers which are acquired by his system are of such a formidable nature that they might be terribly abused if they fell into the wrong hands. He considers, therefore, that the human race is not yet prepared for the just exercise of these forces, and that a great responsibility rests with his order to test every candidate for initiation in the most severe manner, and so to insure that no unworthy man should ever gain admission to the brotherhood. This is the adept's reply, and, right or wrong, he inflexibly adheres to the line of conduct which he has laid down for himself.

For the information which I have jotted down here I am indebted partly to my own reading, partly to what I have heard from my father, and most of all to Mr. A. P. Sinnett, for his excellent summary of the occult philosophy. ("The Occult World." Trübner and Co., 1883.) I cannot supplement my account better than by adding one or two of Mr. Sinnett's clear and forcible statements.

"The whole edifice of occultism," he writes, "from basement to roof, is so utterly strange to ordinary conceptions that it is difficult to know how to begin an explanation of its contents. How could one describe a calculating machine to an audience unfamiliar with the simplest mechanical contrivances and knowing nothing of arithmetic? And the highly-cultured classes of modern Europe as regards the achievements of occultism are, in spite of the perfection of their literary scholarship and the exquisite precision of their attainments in their own departments of science, in the position as regards occultism of knowing nothing about the A. B. C. of the subject, nothing about the capacities of the soul at all as distinguished from the capacities of body and soul combined. The occultists have for ages devoted themselves to that study chiefly; they have accomplished results in connection with it which are absolutely bewildering in their magnificence; but, suddenly introduced to some of these, the prosaic intelligence is staggered, and feels in a world of miracle and enchantment."

In another part of his interesting work Mr. Sinnett deals with sounds produced at a distance by adepts which correspond to those which haunted my father for so long. Of these he has had personal experience. "It is never loud," he says; "at least, I have never heard it very loud; but it is always clear and distinct to a remarkable extent. If you lightly strike the edge of a thin claret glass with a knife you may get a sound which it would be difficult to persuade any one had come from another room; but the occult bell sound is like that, only purer and clearer, with no subsound of jarring in it whatever ... The bell sounds are not mere sportive illustrations of the properties of the currents which are set in action to produce them. They serve the direct practical purpose among occultists of a telegraphic call-bell. It appears that where trained occultists are concerned, so that the mysterious magnetic connection which enables them to communicate ideas is once established, they can produce the bell sounds at any distance in the neighborhood of the fellow initiate whose attention they wish to attract." From my father's case it seems that this bell sound is used not merely for the purpose of communication, but also to enable the adepts to retain their hold over any individual and to inform them exactly where he was that they might lay hands upon him at any moment.

These few additional particulars may throw some light upon any obscure points in the statement which has been so concisely and truthfully drawn up by my friend and brother, John Fothergill West.

THE END.